Love's Aftermath: Can You Stand The Rain?

Written By:
Carrie Farley

Dedication and Acknowledgements

I will ALWAYS thank **God** for allowing me to continue in this writing thing! Lord, I do not take this gift for granted and pray that I always lift you up in whatever endeavors that I choose to pursue.

Frances Marr, aka "Mommie Dearest," again I thank you for your continued support and encouragement to finish book #4!!! You are forever the "Wind Beneath My Wings." I thank God for your life and, most importantly, your love. "You only get one…"

To **My Family**…thank you so much for your patience, understanding, and unconditional support while I was grinding to get yet another project done. I pray one day; this hobby will begin to lay a foundation for added blessings and opportunities for our family.

My BFF since 1st grade, **Janneseka Franklin, aka "Nese,"** and my cousin, **Alyssa Moseley**…. THANK YOU for continuing to be my sounding board and help with editing. I appreciate your ongoing commitment to this project and series overall.

To my Pastor—**Apostle William A. Lash III** of the City of Victory Church, I thank you for your continued support that you had for me and my writing. The messages I had to prepare on Sundays to teach have given me some of the content I use in this series. Thank You eternally!

****This Love Series will always be dedicated to my father, the late and great Boyde L. Marr…Forever a "Daddy's Girl." ****

*Last, but not least, I would like to acknowledge those who have supported this series so far. Whether it was from buying both copies, sharing a post, or telling someone else about the books. You are appreciated!

Table of Contents

Prologue

Kamal and Ondrea had just arrived back home from seeing Coming to America 2 at the movie theater followed by stopping to eat their favorite soul food meal at Chef Vino's restaurant.

"God, you gotta help me...he's looking at me like he wants some," Ondrea silently prayed to herself while trying not to wear her feelings on her sleeve. She quickly removed the pink DKNY button-up shirt dress, underwear, and matching knee-high-heeled boots she was wearing to hurry and put on some flannel pajamas. She didn't even want to take a shower and risk him making any advances. She looked over at the clock, which currently read 7:44pm.

Since the wedding, the newlyweds had been getting it in on the regular—at least six times a week...however Saturdays after 8pm were off limits so that Kamal could fast before he preached on Sunday mornings. The sex continued to be fire since the first time that they first connected, however there were still times where Ondrea's feelings of anger, and unforgiveness of Kamal taking Chance's life reared their ugly head. When this occurred, she could hardly stand to have him touch her, let alone be in the same house with her, and those were the times where she had to pray most.

Kamal knew that forgiving him for his offense and moving forward was a hard task for Ondrea to handle, but she had vowed to work through this with him to fight for their marriage before they officially had even made it down to the altar. He knew that there was no amount of overcompensation he could give both her and Tania to make up for their loss...this was truly a job for Jesus.

He watched Ondrea as she began to wrap her hair up and he rushed over to her side to hand her the scarf she used to tie her hair.

"Thanks," Ondrea returned dryly.

1

"You're welcome, beautiful," Kamal said as he saw the angry scowl on her face, "what's the matter 'Drea? "

"I don't know what you're talking about, Kamal," she replied while turning around to act like she was looking for something.

"Nope, nope, don't start this shut down on me, now…come on and talk to me."

Ondrea gave a huge sigh. Tomorrow was the anniversary of the day she received the phone call that was forever etched in her memory when they found Chance's bullet-laden body in an alley. Better yet, the anniversary of her husband murdering her late husband. *"What have I done?! How could I even think I could ever go through with this in the first place?! God, help me!"* she continued to pray to herself. She fixed her face to match her husband's desire, and then turned around to face him. "I'm fine, babe…trust me," she said as she leaned in to kiss him gently on the lips, "are you needing some more reassurance, Minister?" she teased.

Not forgetting the expression on her face before then, he replied, "now you know I'm gonna need way more than that to put my mind at ease."

"At your service," Ondrea stated as she dropped to her knees and began unbuttoning his pants. He then snatched her up, leaning in to give her a deeper kiss, which turned into more. As they quickly removed each other's articles of clothing, he turned her around and entered her from behind. She began to swallow her tears of hurt with every stroke of pleasure Kamal gave to help erase her pain.

He switched her to missionary position on the bed and began to look into her watery eyes.

"Are you okay, 'Drea?" he asked her with all seriousness between the soft strokes he was giving.

She nodded in agreement, "Yes," she moaned.

Kamal wondered what would make Ondrea want to shed tears the way that she had—she hadn't done that since their wedding night. Whatever the reason, with a nervous and anxious feeling he hoped they were all for the right reason.

"I love you, Ondrea," he stated as he rolled off her and kissed her on the top of her forehead.

"I love you too, Kamal," she replied while burying her face in his chest, "can you hold me?"

"You already know, beautiful," he replied holding her tightly as they fell asleep.

****

"You cheated, 'T!" both Londyn and Tania exclaimed.

"You know you have to draw four more cards when I change the color also," Londyn retorted while playfully hitting him on the leg.

Uno had become their favorite card game to play when Sincere went back to Philly to begin his sophomore year in college, leaving just the three of them. After Tania was released from the hospital up until then, it was Spades.

Just then, they could hear Journey becoming irritable on the baby monitor. "I'll put her down before I head out," Tyrin Jr. said to Londyn as he got up from her living room floor to head to Journey's nursery her grandparents had set up for them. Journey's nursery room was the most blinged out nursery anyone had ever seen. Complete from the entertainment center, mini kitchen to the bathroom added on, no one needed to leave it while caring for her. Whenever Londyn needed a break, 'T was able to stay one night a week and was confined only to Journey's room.

"Thanks, babe," Londyn replied smacking him on the butt and winking at him as he passed. He then gave her back a sneering look, as he never liked her smacking him on his butt while playing around.

"Okay, now," Tania interjected, "I don't need anymore niece/nephew-cousins anytime soon," she said playfully.

"Shut up heffa!" Londyn replied. "You know he only volunteered because he was about to lose."

"I know, he thinks he's slick!" Tania laughed.

"I'm so glad you're staying over tonight...I missed our weekend sleepovers," Londyn stated as she glanced over at Tania's blinged-out walker—she was glad when she had progressed out of the wheelchair and could now spend the night again without all the extra hassle of maneuvering around on wheels. "Progress, Chica! You'll be on that cane for sure come April!" she exclaimed.

This past summer, Londyn never thought that her best friend not only would almost lose her life but be unable to cheer with her during their sophomore year in high school. For starters she was angry with Tania for going with Treasure to that house party from jump, not to mention drinking and then running out in the middle of the street not focused on her whereabouts and just emotion. Londyn was also upset with Sebastian for playing her girl the way that he did...he better be glad that Tania made 'T promise that he wouldn't beat him up. For Tania and Sebastian there were a lot of shoulda-coulda-wouldas involved in that moment, however what was done was done, and the only focus had to be on moving forward.

"Me too, Sissy," Tania replied, "it's been a long time coming, but I know a change gon' come!" she playfully sang in the tune of the infamous Sam Cooke song. "It's so hard being at home and living with the two of them sometimes, you know," she lamented. "I mean, don't get me wrong, Minister Kamal is great for my mom, and I love him for that, but on the flip side, this is crazy how I don't know my daddy because of him...it's like I'm in the Twilight Zone or something at times, Londyn..." she stated as her voice trailed off. She didn't want to cry again today—she already had a rough physical therapy session where she had shed some tears.

"I can only imagine, Tania...I still can't believe he did that. He seems so different than the monster we learned he was...I wonder how many other people know..."

"...No one else knows outside Cousin 'Rin and Pastor Samuels...and Londyn, I hope you haven't told anyone!"

"I haven't, but between you and me he needs to be punished for what he's done, Tania..."

"I know, Sissy, but as much as I hate that I'm even getting ready to say this to you...he's already suffering every time he has to look me and my mom in the face—and that, he's gonna have to do for the rest of his life."

Londyn shrugged her shoulders, "I guess when you put it that way...that is some kind of mental torture, huh?"

Tania nodded in agreement. This summer she had learned the ugly truth about love and loyalty...both are unto death, and she finally understood the meaning of the two words through her mother and Minister Kamal.

"What ya'll two big-heads talking about behind my back?" asked 'T as he came back around the corner scaring Londyn and Tania.

"Dang boy!" exclaimed Tania, "Don't scare us like that!"

"Yeah," agreed Londyn. "You're about to have us wake Journey back up," she added.

"Chill, babe. She's good. She's out like a light," he said while staring into her eyes with his baby blues and cheesing with confidence.

"Okay…" she replied with a hint of skepticism, "just so you know you still have to draw your cards, sir…we ain't forget!" Londyn laughed.

"Ya'll tripping…besides, I'm outta here, I gotta get Pops' Tesla back before he gets home."

"You always doing something you aren't supposed to," Londyn scolded.

"Yeah, but you like when I do what I do to you though," he kidded.

"Ugh…puppies!" Tania stated while covering her ears with a look of disgust on her face.

Londyn playfully hit him in the arm, "Time to go, 'T!" she said as she got up to walk with him to the foyer while he said goodnight to Londyn's parents.

****

Londyn had just helped Tania get ready for bed and left out of her bedroom to check on Journey before retiring for the night. Tania folded up her walker and placed it against the nightstand by her bedside and maneuvered herself into Londyn's bottom bunk. *"I can't believe her parents haven't upgraded her bedroom yet,"* she thought to herself. *"I can't wait on Londyn to come back…I have to get my mind right and prepared for this counseling session tomorrow after service…why'd they set this up after church anyways?"* she said in annoyance.

As she continued to lay there, Tania couldn't help but turn her frown into a smile. She was grateful for her friends. Her boyfriend, Sincere Phillips was also a blessing in her life, and she missed him whenever he had to return to Pennsylvania, where he was a student at Temple University. *"Temporary setbacks for a major comeback,"* she said to herself as she started to drift off to sleep.

Chapter One

"*Better Days, better days, better days are coming...*" Ondrea wiped the tears from her brown almond-shaped eyes as she heard the choir singing. All that was missing was Leandria Johnson herself singing lead in only the way she can.

Her eyes then shifted to her husband, Kamal who entered the pulpit with Pastor Samuels. Ondrea still had a lot to learn in being a pastor's wife, and until Pastor Samuels believed they were stronger as a unit then he would step down and leave the ministry in Kamal's care. Kamal was an anointed preacher, and an even better teacher...she knew without a shadow of a doubt that every time he stepped up to deliver God's Word, deliverance, healing, and the power of God always fell. Given the extreme sadness that she was feeling today, she needed a Rhema Word.

Minister Kamal could feel a tug on his spirit form his wife, and he knew something was going on with Ondrea— *"God, what is it that You would have me to say that will minister not only to Your people, but most importantly my wife?"* he prayed silently. God had revealed to him that he needed to preach something to encourage the people on this morning, and that spirits were heavy burdened and melancholy. As the choir finished their selection Kamal stood up in front of the podium, and then asked the Lord to take lead.

"Praise the Lord, everybody!" he exclaimed. "This is the day that the Lord has made, and we will rejoice and be glad in it...we can't have no rocks crying out for us now!" There were a couple of chuckles, but the congregation was still a little dry.

"That's a little better, now."

Ondrea smiled to herself and thanked the Lord for her husband. She had felt so down, she forgot to even acknowledge God that morning. *"Lord, thank You for sending the Word that I need."*

Minister Kamal continued, "My subject this morning is simply 'Back to the Basics: The Word'…we need a heart of gratitude, ya'll."

"Help us, Lord," Pastor Samuels called out in agreement.

"I'm going to come from 1 Chronicles 16:8-12 on this morning, Saints…in order to be led by God, first we need to obey Him. His Will for our lives is clearer when we obey the things that He wants us to do. You can only find this in His Word…we look here, there, and everywhere for the solutions to our problems, when all we have to do is simply…" Minister Kamal then held up his Bible to signify the ending of his sentence— "The Word."

"Chronicles was written after the children of Israel had been defeated and returned back to Jerusalem. The children of Israel always felt like God had abandoned them and turned His back on them—no different from how some of us may feel at times when disappointments, heartbreak and heartaches come upon us. We can experience things in life that can seem so unbearable and can leave your faith literally shaken and shattered. When this occurs, Saints, the remedy to spark hope again or rebuild and restore purpose and order in your life is in the Scriptures."

"Amen, Minister…take your time, now!" a member shouted out loud.

"Let's look at verse 8…it begins by reminding the people after going through what they went through how David gave thanks and called on God…the people were hurt and felt defeated, but they were brought out and somebody outta praise God for it! Your wilderness experience is almost up…God's getting ready to deliver, so you outta praise Him right now!" The music began to cue up and some people started to praise God.

"Alright now, don't shift me too quick…my help hasn't even come yet," he teased. "Now go with me to verse 9…it continues with action…'sing unto Him…talk of His wondrous works…' when you sing psalms unto God, you're singing sacred hymns…you can only do this when your heart is pure towards our Lord and Savior, Jesus Christ! It's a heart matter ya'll...get your heart right and maybe—just maybe things may work itself out in your favor!"

"Talk about it, preacher!" exclaimed Pastor Samuels.

"Verses 10 and 11 tell us to glory and rejoice...seeking Him continually. Rejoice means to be glad...you can express this through clapping and singing. Ya'll young people always talk about turning up...you can 'turn up' for Christ and have your own praise party how you do best!"

"Alright now!" Londyn hollered out while smiling at Tania. "Girl, he knows he be telling us the truth whether we want to admit it or not," she leaned over and whispered in Tania's ear.

"I'm just saying...praise is contagious if you give over to it!"

"Amen!" Ondrea forced her mouth to give a praise from her lips to defeat the enemy.

"Now let's wrap this on up with verse 12...this verse is important because it tells us to remember four things: 1.) What He's done for you, 2.) How He's brought you through, 3.) When and where He delivered you, and 4.) The mighty works that He's done in our own lives. When you remember these things, then and only then can you sincerely have a grateful heart and thankful praise.... you gotta really mean it, Saints."

There was a hush over the congregation as Minister Kamal knew that his "help" had arrived. "For some of you that are sitting there thinking and in being honest with yourself, you know that your heart isn't right towards God. Some of you are sitting here at this very moment with hatred even for your Creator. I know because I am not above anyone to have not been in that state spiritually before. I'ma help you on today though to get your joy back and focus up."

"Help us, Minister!" cried out another member of the congregation.

9

When it gets so tough and you can't even find the words to say, or strength at times to lift your hands, let alone your head and smile, remember to go back to the basics! Go back to His Word! Psalm 106:1 says, 'Praise Him for He is good, and His mercy endures forever!' The first clause of Luke 22:17 says 'And He took the cup and gave thanks...' Luke

22:19 says 'And He took the bread and gave thanks and brake it...he said do this in remembrance of me!"

A woman got up and started shouting and giving God the praise.

"You see, Saints, when you're mind begin to shift from, *'Why did this happen to me?'* to *'Who am I and what do God's promises mean for me now?'* then you're finally going somewhere in God! When you no longer know what you think you know is where He then gives you that clarity you need in understanding the relationship with a painful past and Your present God!"

"Hallelujah!" another member hollered as she began to shout her way into deliverance. Soon after, a praise break erupted all over the sanctuary, as the Holy Spirit had its way. As Minister Kamal began to take his seat after giving God the praise, the choir erupted into their best performance ever of "To God Be the Glory."

****

Dearron Howard sat in his 2021 Cadillac Escalade, patiently waiting for his wife, Bria to come outside from using the restroom after service. He secretly was glad that his Assistant Pastor had preached in his place for the last couple of Sundays. He just hadn't been feeling "the call" lately. Still struggling with his wife's infidelity that has resulted in a pregnancy where they do not know who the father is, was enough to break his spirit. Every day since he became aware back in May, he had to fake smiles, hugs, and the love he had for Bria in public—no one knowing that behind closed doors was a different story.

He made sure that Bria was okay physically, however, anything outside of making sure her and the baby's health was fine was not his concern. At one point, he and Tyrin's ex, Taylor contemplated having sex together to help soothe each other's hurt from both of their partner's betrayal, but when it came down to carrying out their plans, they couldn't go past the first kiss. As hurt as Dearron was, and wanted revenge on Bria, he loved his wife and could not see himself harming her more than the cold shoulders and no sex punishment that he already was giving her.

"Sorry I took so long, 'D," Bria replied as she opened the car door and began to step up into the SUV.

"You're fine, Bria," Dearron responded.

Bria knew he was still angry with her—especially by the way he called her by her name and used no terms of endearment anymore whenever he talked to her. She missed their connection and most importantly, her best friend. She reached out to hold his hand, then he moved it away. "'D, will you at least consider coming with me to the baby's appointment this Friday? I really need your support."

He returned a look of reproach and said, "Do you know for sure that this is my baby growing in your belly right now?"

Bria's eyes started to well-up with tears, as she bit her lip and shook her head "no."

"Exactly…but you want my support?! Get outta here, you can't be serious."

"Dearron, do you want a divorce?" Bria finally asked.

He shifted in his seat uncomfortably, "What you mean?"

"Just what I said, 'D…you've been so cold to me since you heard the news, and even though I'm not messing with him anymore…"

"…Yeah, you know not to say that name around me…"

Bria glared, "I don't know how many ways and times you want me to say sorry...it's never going to be enough!"

"We finally on the same page now, huh? I didn't say I want a divorce, Bria, but I need time to figure this all out and how to process what moving forward even looks like," he said as he softened his facial expressions.

"I understand and not fighting you on that...January will be here long before we know it...I just pray to God that you can look at me with love in your eyes for me again instead of disgust."

"Well, you're gonna have to pray hard," he stated as they pulled into their driveway.

****

"Pastor Samuels, we want to thank you for agreeing to counsel with us on today...especially on a Sunday."

"It's no problem, Kamal. You are a good son in the gospel, and anything I can do to help aid in strengthening your family, you know I'm here."

"I appreciate it, Sir," Kamal replied.

"Now, what's been going on with you two? Have you done the homework assignment I asked you to complete?"

"Yes, Sir," Kamal and Ondrea both replied in unison and began to hand him their pieces of paper for him to examine. He then looked them over.

"Now, I'm going to hand them back and have Kamal read his first, and then Ondrea's...where's Tania?" Pastor Samuels asked.

"She's supposed to be joining us today via Zoom...I'll shoot her a text real fast," said Ondrea as she quickly typed a message to send on their iPhones.

"Okay, so back to Kamal's response to why he believes you're here on today."

Kamal cleared his throat, "We are here unfortunately because of me and my actions. I don't know how many ways that I can try to make things right, but nothing can bring that man back. The only way he lives on is through his daughter...I messed up horribly. As we approach this day, no one is acknowledging or speaking on the anniversary of Chance's murder—something I had a hand in—Lord knows, my spirit never settled since I had that man killed...of all the murders committed, this one, even then never sat right with me."

Ondrea raised her head and looked up at her husband who was overcome with grief and could not stop weeping. She instantly felt compassion for him and extended her arms around him. "I didn't know you felt that way," she responded as she cradled him like a baby. "Pastor Samuels, is it alright I don't read mine today? All my anger has been because I felt that he really didn't care about taking his life."

"Of course, I cared, Ondrea. It's just something I never liked to discuss. I think of turning myself into the police for what I've done almost every day..."

"No!" Ondrea raised her voice in opposition, "You can't do that to me. I can't lose another man that I love...don't hurt me over again!" she said as she began to sob uncontrollably.

"Well, my work is done here," Pastor Samuels concluded. "Holy Spirit have your way in this meeting. Minister and heal broken hearts, Lord as only You can! There is a Balm in Gilead!" he began to praise the Lord as he left the two of them in the room.

****

"Tania, where are you sweetie? Getting worried... Love, Mom." Tania rolled her eyes while reading her mother's text. It had started snowing, on top of her emotions all over the place. Tania hated the snow.

13

She had Londyn drop her back off at the house. She was not feeling up to facing Kamal on the day of all days. *"Sorry Mom, I can't do a session on today...you know why...it's just too much for me right now. I love ya'll though, real talk."* Tania finished her text response back to her mother.

"RRRRIIIIIINGGGG!!!"

"Hello," Tania said as she answered the phone.

"Hey My 'Sweet T'," replied Sincere.

Instantly she smiled, "Hey babe, I miss you so much...I need to see you...let's Facetime."

"Bet," he answered as he switched the call to video.

"There's that handsome face," she said continuing her smile.

"...Says the beauty on the other end. What's my baby up though?"

"I'm just sitting here watching the <u>Lust</u> Movie on Lifetime..."

"Figures...anything with Tank on it, I know you're watching," he chuckled. "I was just taking a study break and wanted to hear your voice. Christmas break is getting ready to come up, what are you thinking?"

"I want to come and stay up there with you for the break."

"Say less, babe—wait a minute, what's going on with your therapy sessions and everything? That's gonna mess with your progress," Sincere said with a look of concern. He was at the point of proposing marriage to Tania right before her devastating news followed by her accident. He was working his way back up to that moment again, but only in the right timing—God's timing. Sincere knew Tania was end game for him from the moment he saw her when he first visited his grandmother Helen's church. Although he had his pick of women from all grades in high school to all levels in college, his focus stayed on the brown-skin beauty who stole his heart. From the beginning they had an instant chemistry, and when he heard about how she was a virgin, on top of the way her ex, Sebastian had been playing her behind her back with not only his cousin,

Seneca, but others—at that point, he made it his intention to take her from him and make her his.

Tania looked over at her walker and fought back her tears. "I know…"

A smirk came across his face, "Tell you what…how about spend the week down there, and bring you back with me for New Year's Eve?"

"Really?!" Tania squealed, "Hell—I mean, heck yeah! Thank you, baby!" She allowed the tears of joy to flow freely now.

"Don't cry 'Sweet T…'I can't wait to hold you in my arms."

"Aye nigga, quit caking and let's finish studying this physiology bruh!" his roommate, Paco shouted across the room.

"Nigga don't be ignorant while I'm on the phone with my girl," he responded.

"It's cool, baby…get back to studying. I'm glad you were thinking of me."

"Always," Sincere replied coolly as he blew a kiss at Tania's face before hanging up.

"Lord, thanks for the one thing that's going good in my life right now. I love him and I thank You for knowing I would need him during this crazy time in my life. Please forgive me for bailing on Pastor Samuels, my mom and Minister Kamal's family session today. Lord, you gotta help me with this anger and unforgiveness I have towards this man…I want my daddy…wishful thinking, right, Lord," Tania sighed as she drifted off to sleep.

Chapter Two

Everyone was all smiles and laughs on Monday at school. Tania loved that she did not eat in the same lunch period as Sebastian, and that she only had to see him occasionally in the hallways during transitions in between classes. In the middle of all the traffic scurrying in the lunchroom, a classmate approached her.

"Guess who was asking about you since you returned back to school last week?" Tania's classmate, David asked.

"Let me guess, Sebastian?" she said rolling her eyes.

"Yup! He's missing seeing you—"

"—I don't wanna hear all that, Dave!" said Tania shutting him down. "He's the reason I'm even in this state."

"True…just letting you know, friend."

"Thanks, friend," she replied back in a more calming tone.

Tania didn't know why she snapped on her friend the way that she did. She was over Sebastian once she learned that he had been entertaining other girls, on top of sleeping with her godparents' niece, Treasure behind her back. *"I'm so glad I never gave him my virginity. I hate him. That's why I have an even better man…and he's fine…and he treats me way better…F—*

him!" Just then, as soon as Tania looks up, Londyn enters the lunchroom with 'T and Sebastian.

"What the flip is he doing in here?!" Tania demanded.

"I just wanted to see you, Tania," he said sincerely. He stood looking down over her and the mesmerizing smell of his Polo cologne awakened her senses.

"Well, you see me...bye," she said coldly.

Sebastian continued to stare at Tania while everyone else looked at each other with uneasiness at the tension in the room. "I know things between us ended messed up, but just know that I'm a better person and I'm no longer that person I was."

"Great and thanks for sharing," she returned refusing to look him in the eyes.

"Alright, I allowed you this one time...my cousin seems uncomfortable so I'ma need you to bounce," Tyrin stated while pointing over to the door exiting the lunchroom.

"Thanks, man for the chance...Londyn...Tania, I'm here if you need me."

"Bye, Sebastian," she scoffed.

****

"Dude, I'm dead to her..."

"You know what you did to her...I ain't about to pacify you either, nigga...I'm just saying you gotta give that some time. I mean, she still gotta have another surgery in April before she can even start walking on crutches. The only reason I'm still somewhat cool with you is because we are the dream team on that court, and I know you got caught up cause my cousin wasn't giving it up."

Sebastian gave a small chuckle, "Yeah, man...we still young though I didn't know it was gonna affect her like that—"

"Nigga, she was about to give you her goodies...no girl does that unless you're special to her. Why you think that me and that nigga Wayne got beef with each other? Londyn let him up in her first and that nigga salty I gave her a baby and he didn't."

"Guess I never looked at it that way..."

"Until you get married or she get married, if you take her v-card, you gon' always look at her like she's yours. That's your territory."

****

"This outfit is so cute...I wish I knew the sex of this baby already!" Bria lamented. Here she was releasing her stress at Oglethorpe Mall in the baby section at Carter's. As she combed through all the boy and girl clothes, she couldn't help but feel her smile quickly fading. What was supposed to be an exciting time in her life, had turned into a nightmare— one in which she hoped would be over and have a happy ending come January. *"Let me get out of here and just grab my cinnamon pretzel from Auntie Anne's."*

As she made her way out of the store and waddled up to the counter, she heard a familiar laugh behind her. As she turned around, both her and Tyrin had looks of surprise on their faces. He was standing directly in the back of her while holding hands with another woman 5'2," pretty mocha skin, short cut and video vixen frame. His mocha-colored skin looked beautifully flawless, and muscular frame was on display through the gray North Face sweat suit he was wearing. Bria tried not to look down at his gray sweats. His waves were spinning as always.

Tyrin looked around nervously before saying hello, "Hey, Breeze."

"What's up, 'Rin," Bria responded as the other woman looked her up and down.

Immediately Tyrin's eyes traveled from the beautiful face, down to the round belly of his former lover. "How have you been? Francesca, this is my friend, Breeze—I mean, Bria."

"Nice to meet you," Francesca smirked as she began to hug onto her man.

"Likewise," Bria said with confidence. Sensing the jealousy, Bria flipped her hair as it bounced left to right with so much body. *She knows about me;* Bria was convinced by her response.

18

"Ma'am, your pretzel is ready," the cashier interrupted.

"Great seeing you," Bria responded as she turned around, retrieved her pretzel and water, and continued to waddle off. *"What's the chances of me running into this brotha?!"* she sighed. *"As if life can't get any more complicated..."*

****

"Alright, get your fine ass in the house," Tyrin said as he had just finished kissing Francesca, and she was preparing to exit his new toy, the Mercedes-Benz McLaren.

"Dang, she looked good even big and pregnant," Tyrin thought to himself as he shifted his thoughts back to Bria. He enjoyed Francesca's company, but again, he was "Mr.-Feel-Good" to her and a slew of other women who just saw him, his body and wondered what it would do to theirs—nothing more, nothing less. There were times where some caught feelings, but other than Taylor, he never caught them back. Especially if he matched them up to Bria.

Bria was the only woman he knew whose light, caramel complexion literally glossed like honey. Her long, brown naturally curly hair was such a turn-on to him...especially when she attempted to straighten it and the heat caused her edges to curl up. She was slim-thick just like he liked his women, and confident in her appearance, on top of being smart in the books (Accounting that is) and in the streets. They had a good run when they were sixteen trying to make it in life, and they had taken care of each other the best way that they knew how. They had that Tupac and Jada kind of love back then. As far as he was concerned, Tyrin would never meet another Bria Howard that's for sure.

It had been exactly three months since he last saw her at Kamal and Ondrea's wedding. He loved her then and knew that the love was not going to ever leave. She had a man. A whole husband he had admitted to himself, but that didn't count when it came to matters of the heart. He remembered Kamal saying something about the heart being desperately wicked and deceptive one Sunday when he came to visit their church with his son, Tyrin Jr. He tried to put his feelings to the side, but when he found out that she was pregnant and it was a chance that it could be his baby, he saw that as a sign that there could still be hope for them to finally be together—that is until during their last conversation she was contemplating still having an abortion. The conversation was so heated between them that night that he had even contemplated taking Dearron out to prevent her from having to do so. It was Bria herself who persuaded him to leave Dearron alone and go on with his life so that she could be happy with her husband. He picked up his iPhone to call her. *"Dude what is you doing? What if she wit her weak ass husband? You can't blow her up,"* he thought as he switched his mode of communication.

Tyrin began to text instead, **"Hey Breeze, it was good seeing you today. I see you out here rocking pregnancy with grace and beauty. Hit me up when you can...Always..."** he then hit send. *"Here goes nothing."*

Chapter Three

B ria pulled in the garage in her new Mercedes GLA, singing her heart out on the new Muni Long, "Hrs and Hrs" jam. "Then I met you…" she sang before getting interrupted by a phone call…she saw who it was on the caller id: **"Superman."** *Dang! I knew he was gonna do this crap!* Bria looked at her text message. *Let me go on and get this over with.* She began to call him.

"What's good, Breeze?"

"That's disrespectful to text me while you're with your girl."

Tyrin sensed the hint of jealousy in Bria's voice. "No one compares to you, Breeze, and you know this, man!" he finished in his best "Smoky" from the movie, Friday impersonation.

She chuckled, "You silly…but for real, what did you want me to call you for?"

"I know you want to live your fairy tale with Dearron, I get it…but when I saw you, I couldn't help but ask again if I can be involved at all, I mean…what if it's a girl, and its mine?"

"You really have this obsession that it's a girl, huh?"

"Hey, cuz called Tania, and look at your goddaughter…that's all I'm saying."

"Yeah, yeah…I guess."

"Can I see you? Facetime?"

"That might be too much, 'Rin…I'll tell you what, I have a doctor appointment on Friday where I can find out the sex of the baby—"

21

"Say less—I'm there…I mean, unless hubby gonna be there, too. That might be too much drama. I can deal with homie; I just don't need nothing upsetting you and my little girl."

"Sir, you are officially 10-karat crazy," Bria replied laughing. "Believe it or not, he's still not saying too much to me right now…especially these days—"

"Now that the baby's closer to getting here…I get it. I mean, you gotta understand it from a man's standpoint, Breeze. You had another man not only be up in you, but nut in you on top of that and now your baby is the side nigga's?"

"Correction, we do not know if it's your baby yet, and I'd rather not know to be honest."

"That's so selfish, Bria…you know I know; any baby deserves to know who their daddy is."

"I know who the father is, and it's my husband's. Legally it would be his anyways."

"Yeah, whatever…I'll fall back though…what time is your appointment? You still have that doctor you had the last time—"

"I asked you not to ever bring that back up, 'Rin!" Bria shouted. How could he bring up the abortion that she had back when she was pregnant before and didn't know whether that baby was 'D's or Tyrin's then.

"My bad, Breeze, I didn't mean anything by it…swear."

A long pause came in the conversation until Bria finally broke her silence. "It's cool…I'm already just super emotional. I have no support at these visits, and I guess I can use you for that, huh?"

"Superman to the rescue…I got you…always. Text me the details and I'm there."

"Wait a minute, how are you traveling up and down this highway like that and you live in Atlanta?"

"Well, I basically have 'T holding the crib down while I have a construction project down this way I'm working on."

"I'm proud of you, then 'Rin...glad things are looking up for you."

"Appreciate it, baby—I mean, Breeze...you know what I mean," he said smiling.

"Yeah, I get it...bye, 'Rin." Bria hung up the phone with a huge smile spreading across her face. Tyrin always knew how to make her feel that security she longed for from 'D. Why did this situation have to be so complicated. She loved her husband, but this soul tie with Tyrin had to become severed once and for all!

****

Ondrea was stuck in the after-work traffic on I-95. She couldn't call Kamal because he was at the gym during this time. Tyrin and Tyrin Jr. had taken Tania to the movies with them after they got out from school, so they weren't available to chat... She then realized she hadn't talked to Bria in a minute and figured she could check up on her.

"Hey Cow!" she exclaimed.

"Hey Cow," Bria replied.

"What's going on? You sound tired..."

"Just a little stressed..."

"... 'D still giving you the silent treatment?"

"Girl, he is beyond pissed...on top of that, guess who offers to come for support to my doctor appointment on Friday?"

"Well, about time he came to his senses on that. I mean how you gonna preach God's Word harboring unforgiveness to that magnitude? He better be glad gifts are given without repentance, because I bet the power of God still falls when he preaches, too?"

"Girl, he hasn't even been preaching like that lately...even the past two Sundays he's had the Assistant Pastor take over.... but that's not who I'm talking about girl. He wants nothing to do with the baby until he knows for sure it's his."

"That jerk...okay, well, who then?!" Ondrea asked anxiously.

"'Rin...'"

"You're lying! Shut up!"

"I wish I was."

"When did all of this happen? How come you didn't call me?!"

"Literally just hung up with the brotha...I ran into him at Oglethorpe Mall getting a pretzel from Auntie Anne's and doing some retail shopping...you know me..."

"...Yeah, and I know you a little too well..."

"I know where you're going with this, and I promise it's nothing like that. He has a girl and I'm still fighting for my marriage."

"Mmmm hmmm," Ondrea teased, "I mean it...we have a pact, Cow!"

"I know, I know...I'll let you know if it becomes more than feelings of support."

"Okay, now...you better, Chica!"

"In the meantime, you need me to have Kamal try and talk with him?"

"Not yet, I'm trying to give him his space until we know for sure who the dad is. I'm telling you girl; I'd rather not know and pretend this whole scenario never even occurred."

"I can only imagine, honey. Well, no judgement here, just make sure that you do what God tells you to do and not leaning to your own understanding."

"Thanks, girl. I'm just talking," Bria lied. She really didn't want to know and just move on. This one she would just have to take to the grave.

****

Ugh! It seems like I just went to bed! Tania rolled over and hit the alarm and checked her text messages: ***"Hey best fran, and Happy Friday! Please don't be mad at me and T, but we had to take Journey to emergency. She's been up all night screaming at the top of her lungs and started getting a temperature. Sebastian told 'T he could take you to your session after school today. ☺"***

"Just great!" she replied. Suddenly Tania did not feel so good and wanted to just stay home from school.

"Rise and shine, beautiful!" Ondrea said to her daughter as she pulled the covers from over her head.

"Mom! I don't wanna go today…"

"It's because Sebastian is taking you to your therapy session today, right?" her mom said while rubbing her legs.

"I guess everyone knew except me, huh Mom?"

Ondrea began playing in Tania's long, red-streaked hair. "I just found out this morning like you, and Kamal offered to take you instead—"

"Well, why can't we let him do it then, Mom!" Tania protested.

"Because he has to help Pastor Samuels with a funeral situation."

"Fine," she said as she smacked her lips, snatching the covers off the bed and angled herself to get out and get to the bathroom with her walker.

"Make sure you aren't looking too cute," Tania reminded herself. She pulled her hair back into a ponytail and ended up settling for her oversized "Keisha" <u>Belly</u> Movie sweatshirt and matching black and blue leggings from Pop Fit. *"Lord, be with me on today, I don't know what to expect."*

Chapter Four

"Hey, Tania, your parents left the door open for me to come on in if you need help!" Sebastian called out as he entered the Davis Household.

"I'm good, thanks," Tania lied as she struggled coming down the first step with her walker.

"I know you're mad at me, but let me help you…"

"I said I'm good, Sebastian," she insisted.

Sebastian then had no choice but to wait patiently at the end of the staircase for her. He already knew not to go up any further—he knew how quick she was to dismiss him when he snuck into the cafeteria to see her in the lunchroom. *"Damn, I was so stupid to' f' this up,"* he thought to himself. He really loved Tania, but he wasn't ready to commit to her. He knew she was the kind of girl that you wife up, however at seventeen, there was no way that he was ready for that kind of pressure.

She was able to make it to the second-to-the-last step when she lost control of the walker. Sebastian caught her upon solid reflex as she fell into his arms.

"I told you to stop being so stubborn, girl…I got you babe—"

"–Don't you ever call me that again. You lost that right to call me that the minute you started hooking up with Treasure."

"My bad, Tania…I'—I'm sorry."

"Sorry for what, though? The fact that I'm in this freaking walker, or that you screwed her and whoever else?"

"Both," he said as he looked her dead in the eyes as he slowly released her from his hold.

26

Tania didn't know what to do with the apology from Sebastian. She knew it was genuine, however she knew she was not able to trust him further than that. As he helped her out the house and into the car, she appreciated the gentle care and attention that he was giving her. She even paid attention to him long enough to realize he had cut off his man bun. *"Why couldn't he just be right?"* she thought to herself as he began to pull off.

****

"Told you, Breeze!" Tyrin exclaimed as he celebrated with a bright smile displaying his pearly whites and deep dimples. The doctor had just confirmed Bria was carrying a girl, and he was so elated. He then looked at Bria who looked as if she had seen a ghost. "What's up, Breeze? You're not happy?"

She adjusted herself after cleaning the cold ultrasound gel off from her belly with the warm washcloth, "I—I can't believe that you were right, that's all."

"I'm right about a lot of things, Bria...next prediction, is me and you..."

"Don't—don't do that...please, not right now."

"Do what? Tell you how I really feel? Breeze...come on now..."

"...Hold up, does Francesca even know that you are here with me at this very moment?"

"She's a non-factor, Bria...nobody is you. I settle."

"Well, you shouldn't do that to yourself..."

"All I want to do is finally have the family I deserve with 'T, this baby and you as my lady," Tyrin said as licked his lips and reached out to take both Bria's hands into his. "Look at me, Breeze...I got you...look who here—not ole' boy. Ya'll supposed to be for better or for worse, and

27

he somewhere having a 'sucka attack'… can't even man up and be here with you."

"Okay, but we're not going to just sit here bash my husband, though."

"We're not going to tell lies either," he responded as the doctor entered back in the examination room once Bria was fully dressed.

"Sorry to interrupt you two, however I need to let you both know that due to her shortened cervix, Bria needs to make sure she lays down and only get up to use the restroom—you don't want to deliver your little girl too early."

Suddenly Bria became alarmed, "Early?! What's wrong with me?!"

"Now, now dear…no need to panic so soon. Your cervix is short, meaning there's a funneling. This could have occurred through abnormalities in your cervix or uterus, trauma to the cervix or uterus, or even it could be hereditary."

Immediately Bria's mind reflected on the night her mom's pimp came into her room after her mother sold her to him for some crack. He was so rough and even violent with her as he made sure every hole on her body was filled up—not the way any ten-year-old would picture her body having to be handled. *"I was just a kid…"* Bria sighed to herself, holding back tears.

Tyrin immediately picked up where Bria's mind went, and he squeezed her hands in assurance. "Look at me, Breeze…we're going to get through this."

"That's just it, Tyrin…there is no "us," she lamented. "This is a mess," she admitted as she pulled her hands away from his and began to hold her head in her hands.

Her words stung like a million bee stings. "Say what you want, but this little girl is an extension of us…mark my words—that's my baby, Breeze," he finished and walked out the room on her.

"I knew this was a bad idea," Bria admonished to herself. The hold Tyrin had on her was deep at the root and it didn't help that Dearron wasn't here with her—he was instead...*he's always been here for me...Love is patient, love is kind...just stop it, Bria!"*

"Are you okay, ma'am?" the doctor asked.

"I'm just scared that something will happen to my baby."

"Well, you have a supportive partner, so you'll be fine."

"He's not my husband—"

"Well, no judgement zone here," the doctor interrupted her, "I just have a feeling that this guy is in it for the long haul—whoever he is to you."

As the doctor left out from the examination room again, in walked Tyrin. "My bad, Breeze...I keep f—ing up and I don't know how to deal with all this—my feelings about

you, the health of our—I mean 'the' baby...I mean this situation really is some foul shit."

"Exactly, 'Rin...and you cannot act like I am not married. I know me acting like I'm not got us here; however, I've made my choice regardless of if this baby is yours or 'D's...I love my husband."

Tyrin's nostrils began to flare up, "Man, fuck that nigga! He ain't even here and you going through this cervix shit and he ain't the least bit concerned—"

"I just told you to stop disrespecting him and talking about him and he's not here to defend himself."

"You right, you right...I digress. So, am I still allowed to help you to your car? You really shouldn't be driving or operating heavy machinery after she just told you what's up."

Bria wanted to lighten the mood. She knew how angry Tyrin could get. "Sir, yessir!" she teased playfully as she recited one of their favorite lines from the movie <u>Major Payne</u>.

****

Dearron watched from his SUV as Tyrin helped his wife out of the doctor's office and into her car. He then watched as Tyrin closed the car door for her and tapped the top of her hood to her car twice in goodbye while she drove off. Dearron knew he was in there with her when he decided to surprise Bria and pop up at the appointment and instead seeing Tyrin's Tesla parked in the parking lot. *"Lord, help me...I want this man dead and out of the way!"* he thought to himself as he stared at his glove compartment seething with anger. *"What does she see in him anyways?"* He made sure he didn't open it up to reveal the Glock 9 that he had purchased from

his twin, Dane's brother-in-law. He was discreet while he followed closely behind them. *"Lord, who have I become? I don't feel Your presence anymore...help me!"* he prayed to himself for a way of escape from what he wanted to do while in his flesh.

"BRRRIIIINNNNGGGG!" *"Saved by the ring,* "he sighed in relief as he saw Kamal's name come across his screen.

"Bruh, I thank you for calling me before I did something stupid."

"What you mean, brother...something stupid, like Taylor?"

"How did he know that?" he wondered. "Naw, man...you are tripping, Kamal," 'D said with a nervous laugh, "nothing like that at all."

"Then killing Tyrin, huh?"

"Okay, now you're freaking me out big bro—like, how do you know this stuff?"

"I told you man, I actually talk to and go to God about my friends...plus, 'Drea also hinted at her girl still getting the silent treatment from you."

"I knew it man—"

"Naw, bro...so, I figured you not getting no booty from your wife—and you know what they say about pregnant box, so you have to have the wrong mindset right now, and that's only going to lead you to the wrong spirit where you will find yourself doing one of two things: revenge...by sleeping with Taylor, or murder...annihilating your competition."

"You're good ..." Dearron confirmed.

"Nah, it's nothing like that, I just used to be in 'the life' and you got that look in your eyes...familiar spirit, that's all."

"Dang, for real?"

"Straight like that, bro...I'm here to pray with you...you already know. Check out my last service on the church website, man...I believe it'll bless you...let me also guess that you stopped preaching as well?"

"Something like that..."

"Come on and get back right brother...I don't want to see you go down that road—trust me, it's a long crawl back." Just then Kamal's line beeped in with Ondrea on the line. "Sorry brother, I have to take this, she just texted me saying I need to rush home and handle mine...I suggest brother you handle yours. You don't want no one else to get there before you."

"That's just what happened bro—"

"What you mean—dude was in your bed?!"

"Naw, naw...nothing like that, but he was at the doctor's appointment with her though—"

"I told you man…you need to be smart about this. You have another man actively at your wife, bro…you are giving the enemy all kinds of space and opportunity to divide and conquer that…do you love her?"

"Yeah, man," Dearron said with defeat in his pride.

"Then fight for her…" Kamal looked at Ondrea calling him again, "…Alright brother, I got an emergency I need to take care of. Take my advice and just love her down, bro—you can Cash App me my offering later," he chuckled as he proceeded to click over.

****

Dearron pulled over in the neighborhood library parking lot, pulled up Destiny to Faith Ministries' website on his iPhone and pressed play on Kamal's latest service, "It May Look Like I'm Surrounded, but I'm Surrounded by You." After listening to his thought coming from Isaiah 26:3, he realized in God was where he would experience the peace that passes all understanding.

He kept listening, really trying to receive what his friend and brother in the gospel had to say. "Lamentations 3:21-23 says 'This I recall to my mind; therefore, I have hope. It is of the Lord's mercies that we are not consumed because His compassions fail not…they are renewed every morning, so no matter how long your huge mass of problems and battles you are facing are trying to drag you down, God is right there! You can't control everything so you might as well cast them cares and praise the one who can!"

Dearron began to tear up being re-filled with God's spirit. He continued to listen to Kamal's sermon. "I'm not the only one who's been through trying to shake the spirit of heaviness. In those moments, I thank the Lord I realized I had lost sight of who I was, and the God that I serve. Psalm 119:164 reads, 'seven times a day I praise You….' If we are operating as the Word says, we'd have no room to get the wrong spirit because it's too much praise on our lips, too much joy in our hearts from being grateful, too much peace from The Word penetrating our minds and hearts that we might not sin against it."

Dearron began to praise God. He HAD to keep him mind stayed on Christ. Feeling encouraged, Dearron locked up his glove compartment, and smiled, "*Thank You, Lord for always being so faithful. Please forgive me of my sins I've committed in allowing hurt, anger and pain to overshadow the great commission I've been charged with as a husband as well as a Pastor and most importantly—Your child. In Jesus' Name, Amen!*"

He then picked up his phone to call his wife, "Bria?" he asked as she answered the phone.

"Hey 'D…I didn't expect for you to call me. I just got home from the doctor appointment…I really wish you could've been there with me."

"Yeah, I—uh…I thought about coming up in there, I just—I'm not ready, Bri…"

"You called me 'Bri!' You haven't called me that in a while."

"There's a lot of things I have not done lately, but I'm getting back around to the old me again."

"Well, you already know how I feel about that. I can't wait until our life can go back to some type of normalcy."

"…You think you'd want to watch a movie with me when I get home?"

"Cool with me…I do have to let you know what the doctor said—"

"Bria, I'm really trying, please don't bring that back up—"

"I have to go on bedrest until I give birth," she rushed in, cutting him off.

"What happened?!" Dearron nervously shifted around in his driver's seat while asking with concern.

Bria's face become sullen, "they said that my cervix is short, and it has to be from the trauma I experienced when I was younger," she let the tears start to fall.

Immediately, he wanted to hold her in his arms. Hurt people definitely hurt people through their own selfishness. He was ready to learn more about his wife. It would sure help him to drop the unforgiveness. "Don't cry, Bri...I'm on my way."

****

Ondrea was getting frustrated with Kamal not picking up his phone. Unless there was something at the church that came up, Kamal never missed her calls.

"First off, Lady...Dearron had an emergency, and I was just wrapping up my conversation with him while you were calling...you need me babe?"

"I need you in the worst way, Minister...I've committed some awful sins and need to confess—"

"Not good, Sis. 'Drea... I'm gonna have to baptize you again...maybe this time it'll take."

"Hurry, I need for this problem to be taken care of..."

Kamal put his foot to the pedal and proceeded to speed all the way home. He loved when Ondrea switched it up sometimes and engaged in role-play. "Yeah, and you going to scream in deliverance when I give it to you...get that jacuzzi ready, I'll be there in fifteen."

****

"Ahhh, Kamal!" Ondrea cried out in pain.

"Sorry, babe...too hard? Deep? What?!" he knew she'd scream, but not that kind. Kamal then looked down and instantly became alarmed. "Babe, first thing's first...I'm gonna need for you to not panic, and I'm

34

going to help you get out of the jacuzzi now," he directed as he began to see numerous bright, red globs start to appear in the water.

"Kamal, what's going on with me?!" she asked in agony, as she finally looked down and was able to see the blood too. As he picked her up out of the jacuzzi, the pain intensified and became ten times worse than before. She didn't want to worry Kamal, but she felt very faint and light-headed…and just like that, she was out.

Chapter Five

"*L*ord, protect my wife from whatever is going on!*"* Kamal silently prayed to himself as he rode alongside Ondrea in the ambulance.

The waiting room experience was the most crucial for him. Some months prior, both he and Ondrea were in this situation with Tania. Whatever was going on with her was serious enough for him to alert Tania, but at the same time, until he knew for sure what was going on, he did not want to alarm her.

It was just him alone for the next four hours until the hospital staff called him back to be able to see his wife.

"I appreciate you taking care of my wife, sir," Kamal sincerely thanked the doctor.

"No worries, Mr. Davis…so, the good news is that your wife is doing great. I'm glad that you were able to get her here when you did—"

"Well, what was the issue?" Kamal demanded.

"Well, we had to perform a slight emergency surgery…you may or may not have known this, but she was about three months pregnant when she began miscarrying. We were able to do a small procedure to remove the remaining tissue and remains."

"D—Did she know this, Doc?" Kamal stuttered while questioning. His eyes began to well up with tears.

"No, not at all. She probably just thought she may have been having her irregular periods—I saw in her chart history that she has those—that's probably what made her unaware…I'm so sorry."

"Will we be able to try for another baby in the future?"

"I believe so, Mr. Davis," he answered as they both looked at Ondrea sleeping peacefully. "Right now, I would just focus on getting her through this part and I will keep you two in my thoughts."

"Thanks, Doc," returned Kamal. He looked down at his sleeping wife. "I love you, baby." He replied, gently stroking Ondrea's cheek. *Everything associated with me in her life equals death—Lord, why do I bring her so much pain? Did I make the right decision? Should I have just left her alone?* He held back his tears that were slowly starting to form. He had to remain strong for her at this point. His feelings could wait.

Kamal wanted badly to be a father of his own child with his wife. While he had countless sexual escapades with a plethora of baddies and professional women over the years, to his knowledge he never managed to get anyone pregnant. Kamal never settled down with any woman past two hook-ups to prevent himself from getting attached. There was only one woman with whom he'd double-backed twice, but there was no chance in him fathering a child with her

due to her being murdered during a shoot-out where both he and Big Cash were the targets. The aftermath of her tragic death left Kamal swearing that he would never deal with women again until he was ready for marriage. Ondrea always told Kamal that she found it hard to believe that he had never been in a long-term relationship before her, because before the ugly past reared its head, he had been the perfect male suitor and remained such a gentleman with her during their courtship.

"Hi…" Ondrea said groggily as she began to open her eyes. "What happened to me?" she asked Kamal as she looked around nervously from the IV in her arm, to the four walls of the hospital bedroom, and then back at Kamal.

He sighed, "I don't know where to begin, but the doctor said that you were pregnant and had a miscarriage, babe."

Immediately, Ondrea's hand covered her open mouth in shock. "How did I not know I was pregnant?" She thought back to the conversation she had when Bria disclosed her pregnancy to her, and she shared the indiscretion her and Kamal had. *Oh, wow...she* **was** *right!* This baby was indeed conceived the night that Kamal showed her who he was behind the man in the clergy collar and preacher robe.

"The doctor said that it's possible for women not to know during their first three months...so, how are you feeling about all of this?" he asked concerned about his wife's mental state.

"I—I'm okay. I want a baby with you, honestly...just not so soon. I want us to enjoy being together first for a while, you know?"

"I understand, Lady."

"What about you, Sir?" Ondrea asked her companion. She didn't want to forget about him or his feelings concerning their situation.

"I'm fine, 'Drea," he stated. "I promise I am. I believe in order, and our family needs to be on one accord before God will see fit to bless us in that way."

"Agreed, babe," she added. "But please, don't tell Tania."

"We can't make keeping secrets from her a habit, 'Drea," Kamal lamented.

"I know, I know...but technically she doesn't have to know about this."

Kamal pulled the hospital blankets back to reveal two small bandages over Ondrea's stomach, "You're forgetting this slight problem."

"Oh no!" Ondrea shrieked in pain as she touched the bandages on her belly.

"Don't worry, it was a minor procedure they performed on you, and you get to go home tomorrow. You should only be down for about a week...two tops. Don't worry, I got you, Lady...you already know."

"I know, Kamal. Thanks, so much for being you."

"For you, it's no worries babe, that's the easy part," he replied as he kissed Ondrea on her forehead before heading out towards the lobby to allow her to get some more rest, and also to inform Tania.

****

"Ouch!" groaned Tania as she stumbled in soreness to get inside of Sebastian's car. While he had one of the new SUVs by Audi, she still needed assistance getting up and into it.

"My bad, Tania...I probably should have drove my dad's car today."

"No, it's fine. I appreciate you volunteering to take me in the first place. I want to be able to walk as soon as possible, so no pain—no gain."

"I'm so sorry, Tania," Sebastian replied feeling real guilt.

"Will you stop apologizing?!" Tania replied annoyed, "I don't want to keep focusing on what happened, Sebastian. We can't move forward staying stuck."

"Says the very person who also won't forgive me—"

"Don't you dare go there!" Tania fumed as he helped fasten her seatbelt and closed her door.

"What you mean?! Tania, we're young and I just got caught up. I felt as long as I didn't come to you and continue pressuring you for sex that that was cool."

"You couldn't just wait for me? If I was supposed mean that much to you, you would have been able to do that."

"Baby, I was selfish—"

"I told you to address me as Tania, please...we are not together anymore the minute you decided to give your best parts to other girls."

"Best parts? My dick is not my best part, Tania…well, lemme take that back," he said with a smirk.

Tania playfully punched him in the leg, "Boy stop! You are crazy!" she laughed.

"I knew I'd get you to crack that beautiful smile sooner or later…. nah, but seriously, no cap…my best part is my heart, Tania. You'll always have that. On my dead granny, you got that on lock."

"Shut up, Sebastian. You just talking…your penis is also a part of that package in case you missed that memo," she added while rolling her eyes.

Just then, the phone began to ring. Tania looked at the caller ID to recognize her stepfather's number. *I need to remember to save this number.* She thought to herself. *I wonder what he wants anyway…I hope Mom didn't tell him about why I skipped counseling.* She put the phone back in her Kate Spade clutch purse, letting it go to voicemail. She would check the message as soon as Sebastian dropped her back off at home.

"That's your mans…that's why you ain't answer your phone?"

"Don't start, I just didn't want to answer the phone!"

"Why not? I mean, we don't belong to each other anymore, so you don't have to have any shame in your game—"

"Boy stop! What are you even talking about?!" she returned defensively. "This is another one of your mind manipulation tactics, and I ain't going."

Sebastian was infuriated that Tania called his bluff. He knew he was out of pocket to question her, but he still cared. He still loved her. He had learned about Sincere's plans to cuff Tania permanently while he was messing with Seneca. He could have died when he heard the news, on top of learning she was the family member of his competition.

"Man, ain't nobody worried about that clown. Your heart is with me, and I know it, Tania…" Sebastian stated while grabbing her chin to force her into looking in his eyes. His gaze was as serious as he had ever been. "You may be fooling everybody else, but you're not fooling me."

"Whatever, can we change the subject, please?" she replied feeling very uncomfortable now when she saw him lick his lips. They were extra pink too...out of all the times she saw him around school they had never looked like that since they had broken up. *Stay focused.*

With at least ten more minutes before he was going to pull up at her home, Sebastian was stirring up feelings in Tania that were supposed to be gone. She was happy with Sincere. Afterall, he was the perfect catch.

"Okay, I'll stop...so, can we talk about what you want to eat at Waffle House because a brotha is hungry, and your cousin and Londyn are already there."

"What?! I wasn't expecting to be at a restaurant or anything...look at me and how bummy I look right now!"

"Ba—Tania, chill out. You already know you one of the coldest out here."

Tania smacked her lips and rolled her eyes. *He better act like he knows,* she silently thought to herself.

"It'll be like old times...come on...pretty please?" he began to beg playfully.

"Alright, alright...but you have to carry me inside because after that session, you already know my legs are on fire."

"I got you," he replied coolly.

****

As he entered the living room, Dearron found Bria sleeping under the cozy Ugg throw on the new Love sac he had purchased for her to lounge on when she entered her third trimester of pregnancy. Dearron wasn't the least bit bothered by the baby growing in his wife's stomach. On the contrary, he felt the opposite. If only he knew the baby, she was carrying

41

was in fact his, then he could let his excitement show. Until then, he felt that he had to keep his feelings under wraps.

He continued to stare at her in awe of her beauty until she began to stir. "Hey beautiful," he replied with a warm, genuine smile.

"Hey, Babe," she replied pleasantly surprised at her husband's greeting. "How long have you been home?"

"Not long. I wanted to watch that movie with you before I had to start studying for Sunday Service…did you have a movie already in mind that you've picked out?"

"What?! I'm proud of you getting back to preaching again. I miss hearing The Word from you."

"Thanks, like I said, I'm trying Bri. Kamal text me info about this preacher's convention that he wants me to attend with him next week that he just found out about…I'm gonna have to get back in the swing of things if I'm going—oh wait, you're on bed rest…"

"I know, babe. I was hoping that I could get 'Drea to spend some 'sister time' with me while I was on bed rest…I can call and ask her. You go. It would give her some time to spend with 'Noah and I know she wouldn't mind helping me out with him while you're gone."

"You sure, babe?"

"I'm sure, 'D. Now what movie are you thinking of?" she continued.

Dearron stopped to think about his choice. *Funny or Drama? Mystery or Romcom?* "Genre-wise, what are you in the mood for?"

"Ummm…let's watch something serious that we can discuss afterwards."

"Okay, how about <u>Really Love</u> with your boy, Kofi in it?"

"Yes, I've been wanting to check it out."

"Him or the movie?" he said with a chuckle.

42

"If I tell you, I gotta kill you," she said with a hearty laugh.

Dearron grabbed some Fiji water bottles and bag of Mike Sells Puffcorn and plopped down on the sectional next to where Bria sat. He then found and pressed play on the movie. When the movie was over, they both couldn't help but dive into conversation surrounding the overall theme of the film—not being afraid of who you love, and the feelings that may come from loving that person. They went on for over an hour discussing the points of parents having such a heavy influence (good or bad) on their children, to even how people settle in relationships.

"So, tell me Bria," Dearron inquired of his spouse, "what was it like growing up the way that you did prior to me meeting you?"

Bria sighed. She didn't want to do this right now, but if she was going to open to anyone about her past in detail, it would have to be her husband…they were on a good path now, and she wanted nothing to get in the way and stop it. "It was really, hard for me Dearron. I had my own father pimp my mother out to his boys…" she gulped, as a lump of pain in her throat started to form. Dearron was there this time to be her shoulder she leaned on and held her as she started telling him her memories of growing up as the tears began to fall.

"You're safe with me, Bria. I'm sorry for making you feel anything other than that. You don't have to continue if you don't want to…"

"No, it's alright, 'D'…I owe you this truth. For over six years I was molested and raped by over eleven men—including my father, cousin, and uncle. My father would continue to pimp me out to his friends, and my mother helped him. She helped him so she could get her drugs."

Dearron continued to pay close attention to Bria as she described that period in her life. She discussed the fact that she had already had two abortions by the time she started high school, and one of the baby's was from her uncle that paid her mother regularly for sex with her.

"When did all of this stop for you?"

"Honestly, when I was supposed to have ten guys run a train on me, one of the guys in that train saw the look in my eyes and convinced everyone else not to go through with the service."

"I'm happy to know that man looked out for my future wife."

"I'm glad you're saying this now, because after that happened, my pimp became very upset and wanted to kill him. The guy got to him first, and the rest is history."

Dearron was starting to put two and two together. "Bri, can I ask you another question? And answer it truthfully…"

"Don't do me like that, babe," Bria pleaded.

"Is the guy you're referring to, Tyrin?"

"Yes."

"So, that is what's so special about him…the fact that he saved your life?"

"In so many words…yeah, I guess that would be it. Also, with him coming from that life, he understood me and my battles and demons that I had to fight. He helped me through some dark times in my life…nothing more and nothing less."

"Except you left out the sex part."

"'D, now you know I don't feel comfortable discussing sex with him to you."

"Okay, fair enough…so, do you believe that I really am your soul mate, and that you're not settling with me?"

"Baby, I'm very sure. I know beyond a shadow of the doubt that you are the man for me. You literally complete me. I would be most miserable if there wasn't a 'you and me'…I've loved you since age seventeen, I'd say that's noteworthy, what about you?"

"Bri, you're the truth. I loved you since I first laid eyes on you. Now, you were with Dane at the time, so I had to fall back for the time being—you know, my brother and I were used to getting that 'No Limit' Cane and Abel action."

"No way!" Bria screamed.

"Yeah, that's how that went. When you started playing those video games with me, our conversation picked up, and I had to shoot my shot...I didn't care about anyone else who might've been involved at that point."

"Yeah, what was up with Joanna saying something about you were seeing someone on the low—was that true?"

"At the time it was an off and on thing with my tutor for about eight months, but it was over for sure by the time we hooked up. Once you turned me out, it was a wrap." He said with a smile.

"Please, you were the one schooling me with the ice..."

"You remember that, Bri? Wow!!!!" he replied shocked.

"Wow, we're learning a lot of things about each other as life progresses, aren't we?" Bria confirmed.

"Well, that was the goal, right?"

"True, true...I'm just saying, we all have growing up to do. I can't erase what I've done 'D, but I can try. I really am not attached to him like that."

"So, you're telling me that if I would allow a threesome with you, me and him you would turn it down?"

Bria's jaw dropped in complete shock at her husband's proposition, but immediately the corners of her mouth turned up into a grin. "You're joking, right?"

"Look at my face…I can't believe you'd think I would really be into that," he stated disappointed.

"But we've invited women in before, that's why I didn't think anything of it when you said that—you're acting as if we've never done threesomes at all!"

"A man does not want to see another man enter into his wife or see her pleasuring another man though…"

"…And you think a woman wants to see her husband enter another woman or hear her screams and moans? Come on now, you had your fun with Marie…you really think I enjoyed that?"

"Okay, we weren't bringing 'Drea's cousin in this though…I see your point, but I'm really trying here because I love you, Bria. Him though? You might be carrying this niggas baby and you're basically telling me that you aren't done with him because you want him in a ménage-trois with us? I'm not doing it, Bri."

"Sometimes I miss before you became a pastor…you know how we do it, 'D."

"Yeah, but that usually ends in me giving you this 'D'…no one else." he added in.

"Oh yeah?" Bria responded.

"Let me stop because you can't do anything with the short cervix and bedrest, right?" Dearron felt salty because he was so angry all this time with Bria that he forgot how sexually frustrated he had been.

"Come here, baby I wanna whisper something to you…"

"As many times as, you have watched that movie, I'm not falling for the Poetic Justice quotes, Bri!" he responded with laughter.

"Shut up and come here, 'D!" she commanded. Her eyes seductively luring him back over to her as she sat back up in the Love sac.

"Wait a minute, where's 'Noah?!'" he asked, suddenly inquiring about their son.

"Dane and Treasure came by to grab him. We have the evening to ourselves—and with no evening service, praise the Lord!" she said jokingly.

"Don't do God like that!" he said.

"Relax, 'D...'" she said as she tugged at his shirt, playfully pulling him over to her until he was standing over top of her. "Don't be so hard on yourself...no pun intended." She smiled in satisfaction while looking at her husband's response to her advances. It had been so long since she was able to get this kind of reaction from him, and she was going to take full advantage of it.

Dearron closed his eyes and moaned in ecstasy as Bria unzipped his pants and proceeded to work on him. Truthfully, no one put it down better than Bria. He had to admit to himself, as much as he wanted to be upset with Tyrin for applying so much pressure on Bria to be with him, he understood why. When she finished blessing her husband, he graciously got down on all fours as she lay back down, to eagerly returned the favor to her. Both of their faces glistening as they had made a new connection relishing in each other's responses to their expression of love and the need to fulfill the void their bodies lacked...pleasure and intimacy.

Chapter Six

"And that's why your head is so big you don't have dreams, you watch movies!" Sebastian stated as he and 'T exchanged cracks on each other.

"Man, you so stupid, you snuck on the bus and paid to get off!" 'T returned.

Everyone busted out laughing. This is what everyone missed deep down…the "Fabulous Four" were all back hanging together again like old times. The last time they were all together, was a couple's date night at the movies and axe-throwing. 'T and Sebastian were both very competitive, while Tania and Londyn were foodies, so their dates usually consisted of both restaurants and something that involved keeping scores.

"It's good to see you laughing, cuzzo," stated 'T. He was so glad to get his cousin out the house and amongst friends again. Truth of the matter was that although Tyrin was cool with Sincere and like how he treated his cousin, he longed for Sebastian and Ondrea to work it out. He knew that she was deeply hurt by him, and that Sebastian really cared for her—they were just too young for something serious.

"Yeah…it feels good to get out and about. I can't wait to get on this cane…that equals getting closer to walking without any assistance…I can't wait for the finish line."

Then, awkward silence occurred as everyone quickly glanced over at Sebastian, who began to look over at the countertops to divert the attention brought on him. He then glanced back at everyone, pointing out Ms. Debra Antney, successful businesswoman, and rapper Wacka Flocka's mother who was waiting for her order at the counter. They all proceeded to wave and say hello to her, and she waved back in return.

Atlanta was full of good people, with celebrities who still showed how down-to-earth they were whenever they may have encountered young people who were star-struck, or just genuine fans.

Tania's cell phone began to ring again. She looked down and for the third time, it was Kamal. *I better answer this*, she thought as she began to think it must be very important for him to continue calling like this. "Hello?" she answered hesitantly.

"Tania! Thank God I was able to reach you...I've been trying over the past couple of hours."

"I'm sorry, I just looked at my phone," she partially lied.

"I'm just glad you're okay...well, let me cut to the chase...I'm here at the hospital with your mom—"

"...What?! Which one?! What's going on?!" she demanded.

"Calm down for a sec, she's fine. I'm here with her. She will be home tomorrow, and we can talk to you then about what happened. For now, your mother needs to know that you are going to remain calm so that she can stop worrying about you."

Tania sighed, "can you at least tell me what hospital she's in?"

"I'm sorry baby girl, she made me promise not to tell you all that...I barely convinced her to tell you the truth."

"Yeah, that sounds like her," Tania chuckled.

"You know her better than anyone."

"Well, can you give her a big hug and kiss for me? Thank you for looking out for her. I meant what I said about you being good for my mother, it's just the other stuff—"

"I know, I know...and with God's help we can get through it, Tania. I really and truly am sorry that you're having to deal with all this. It's never sat right with me since the day I did it."

49

"Really?" she asked surprised. She had just known that Kamal felt no remorse for murdering her father.

"Yes, but we can talk about it more if you like after your mother gets home. I'm going to head back into her room now and make sure that she's getting rest like she's supposed to...sounds like you're with company."

"Oh yes, me and Londyn, 'T and Sebastian are at Waffle House."

"Sebastian?"

"Yeah, like you said, we can talk when you and mom get back."

Kamal chuckled to himself, "Alright, baby girl...as you wish."

"Bye-Bye," she returned as she hung up the phone.

"Everything alright?" Londyn asked Tania.

"It's okay, my mother is in the hospital for some reason though, and Minister Kamal isn't disclosing where she is because my mom asked him not to. She'll be home tomorrow though, he said."

"Whoa, are you okay, Tania?"

"I'll be alright once I see her, but at least he assured me that he's staying with her."

"Well, where are you going to stay then if they're gone?" Sebastian asked.

"She can stay with me and my dad overnight, right Tania?" 'T rushed in as he winked at his cousin with a smile.

"Sure, I can text him back and let him know to pick me up from your house tomorrow."

"Okay, bet. Thanks for helping us out with her today, Sebastian. Real talk, you came through clutch and that means a lot."

"No doubt," he said looking across the table at Tania. "Even though I may have lost her to someone else, I will always look out for her and her best interest."

"Awww!!!" Londyn teased as 'T imitated violin strings being played. Tania remained silent—not knowing how to respond.

****

Bria woke up with severe hunger pangs. It was a couple hours later, and 'D was in his study trying to get back into the swing of things by reading The Word. She ended up ordering both a Cap'n Crunch smoothie from Fit Lab coupled with amazing dinners from Wright's Soul Food through Door Dash. *Boy, I wish Sunday's Eatery was up here in ATL,* she thought to herself as she remembered the bomb soul food, she received at Trick Daddy's tasty establishment. *He can eat one of these meatloaf dinners...I can't wait to dig my hands in this scrumptious food,* she thought. Here she was with two to three weeks left in her pregnancy, and she was going to have to be confined to their guest suite on the main floor with no wheels to push, and idle time.

I should call Tyrin and tell him I'm good now...no, just 'ghost' him! But he's been so supportive...girl, that's what got you here in this entanglement already... you better not call him! Bria picked the phone up, and instead called Ondrea.

"Hello?"

"Hey Cow!"

"Hey Cow!" a voice answered back that obviously was not Ondrea.

"Kamal?!" Bria demanded.

"Yes, sis," he returned with laugh.

"Boy, you better put my girl on the phone!" she said returning the laugh.

"Yeah…uh, I wasn't going to tell you this, but we're at the hospital right now. She should be getting discharged to come home later today, and I can call you back when she gets situated."

"What happened, Kamal?!"

"I don't know if I should tell you while you're still pregnant."

"Is she going to die?!"

"No, calm down, Bria." he said firmly. "She had a miscarriage and had a small procedure done…"

"…She didn't say anything to me about being pregnant. How far a long was she? Oh man, I hate to hear this."

"Well, the doctor said with her irregular periods she may not have known, and that she was approaching the three-month mark."

"How are you guys holding up?" Bria felt so bad for her friend and Kamal.

"Right now, it's the initial shock…we're still trying to process this, but God is faithful."

"I'm glad that she has you for strength. Listen, while I have you on the phone, 'D showed me the info on the preacher's convention in Macon next week. If you are still going, maybe it won't be such a bad thing if 'Drea comes and stays here with me. Hopefully the time with her bestie may give her some comfort and support."

"That's a good point, Bria. Both 'T and Tania are supposed to go visit with Sincere, plus we'll be back on Christmas Eve…so just in time for Dearron to make it back to give you all your presents and everything— it'll be cool. I'll run it past her once we get home, and again I'll make sure to have her call you."

"Sounds good, brother. Thanks for letting me know what's going on also."

"No worries, sis."

****

As everyone said their goodbyes to Sebastian and exited in 'T's car, 'T couldn't help but probe his cousin to see where her head was. "So, cuzzo…inquiring minds wanna know, what's up with you and my boy, 'Bastard'."

Tania chuckled, "You are so silly calling him that, though, 'T…I don't know, I mean its cool that he apologized, and I actually believe he's sorry, but it ends there."

"Say less then, I'll leave that alone," he added. "By the way, did you text Kamal, yet? I have a slight change of plans."

"What do you mean? And no, I was waiting until we got to your house before I texted him…why, what's up?"

"Well, I need to stop at California Pizza Kitchen in Lennox Mall and pick up me and Londyn's 'Take and Bake' Jamaican Jerk Chicken pizza."

"Oh. I'm not a part of that, huh?"

"You may want something else when we get there."

"But my legs hurt, ya'll. I can't walk up in there…you are teasing me going to the mall, too…and you know I love the mall!" she said with disappointment.

"Okay, okay…I'll run in and grab the pizza and you and Londyn can stay in the car. I'll park right out front, and Londyn can move the car if the security come around and say we have to move."

"Whatever, Tyrin," Londyn and Tania both reluctantly agreed.

About fifteen minutes passed while both girls sat in the car trading conversation surrounding their "boos." Tania spilled her heart to Londyn about how she was starting to have some old feelings for Sebastian stir, but how much she really loved Sincere. She knew with him that it was genuine because they never had any sexual encounters—they had never even been past first base before he went back to school this past semester.

Londyn in turn began to spill the beans to Tania on how much she appreciated her cousin stepping up with helping take care of Journey, however she was starting to become worried that they wouldn't make it as a couple due to Tyrin's rising popularity on the basketball court.

"Girl, him and Sincere done came up with a plan to let him come up to Philly with you the week of New Year's, and as much as I'm excited for him to get a taste of college life, me and Journey is no where a part of that vision…at least not right now, and that scares me."

"I hear you, Sissy, but you know you have my cousin wrapped around your finger, girl."

"Yeah, but he's gonna be up there around all those college girls—"

"…Hold up, Sis! You're the only Seventeen-year-old I know who has had a baby, not have any stretch marks, not to mention stomach back tight after your first two weeks of breast-feeding…Ms.-Had-a-Baby where?! Besides, you know I'm up there also…he ain't stupid," Tania laughed.

"I love you friend," Londyn replied in appreciation. "I needed that pick me up."

"That's what friends are for, just do me a favor and give me a heads up the next time you recruit Sebastian to be my ride to therapy, though."

"My bad, Sissy…we really had no other choice, and besides we knew he wouldn't turn down an opportunity to be in your presence."

"True that!" Tania agreed.

A few more minutes passed. "I'm about to call this brotha…he done went in there and forgot all about us!"

Just as Tania reached back into her clutch to retrieve her phone to call her cousin, he finally emerged fresh out of the pizza place with another young man about three inches taller than him with some Louis Vuitton bags in tow. When she saw his mocha brown complexion, earring in his nose with deep waves—360s spinning, she knew immediately who was in town.

"Sincere!" Tania yelled out of the car window as she tried to open the door.

Realizing what she was trying to do, Sincere broke his stride to rush to her aid. He opened her car door and planted a big kiss on her lips. "Hey, My Sweet T," he added with the biggest smile.

"Baby, how long have you been here?!" She asked.

"Not long. I hit 'Rin up while ya'll were still at Waffle House and he told me what was going on with your moms and that you were staying with him and his dad...I'm on my way to my grandmother's house to put my bags and stuff down...did you wanna come with me?"

"Hecky yeah..." Tania turned to Londyn and 'T, "I mean, no offense, but my man is here," she sang.

"You good cuzzo, I knew you wouldn't want that pizza," he said laughing while Sincere left to pull up in his new Range Rover and help Tania out of 'T's car and into his.

"Bruh, that ride is bussin, when did you cop that?"

"It's just a little something I picked up last week." He said matter-of-factly.

Tania eyed him and the car. "Where'd you get the money for this, Sincere?"

"Dang, Sweet 'T...I'm gonna need you to chill on that," he said slightly annoyed.

"Whatever," she returned and proceeded to stare out of the car window.

Tyrin interrupted to break up the mood. "Well, let me know what day we're riding out with you...we already got our plane tickets for New Year's Day in the afternoon, so you shouldn't have to worry about us getting back."

"Bet," Sincere said.

Tania didn't know what Sincere might have been into, but she knew firsthand the effects from having a father and cousin in "the life." Only death or jail is the fruits of that labor, and she did not want to repeat the cycle her mother went through when she met and married Tania's father, Chance Williams. The only keepsake she had from him was a stuffed animal that he had won for her while him and her mother were at a carnival. Her mother was pregnant with her, and unfortunately, Chance never got to meet her due to him being murdered. Her older cousin Tyrin Sr. just got out of jail a couple years ago and finally turning over a new leaf, but still some residue from the streets was still there. Tania prayed her new love would stay focused on school and basketball, and not get caught up by the fast life.

He and Tania rode in awkward silence for the first three minutes, until Sincere broke the silence while at the nearest traffic stop. "Look, the first thing I don't need is you stressing me over my Range, or any other purchases I make when I come here solely to spend time with you, Tania...I need for you to trust me, I'm solid babe. Seriously."

"Okay, Sincere...I'm not playing." She said with suspicion.

"I know you aren't, and I'm not either," his tone softened and his stare into her eyes changed into something rather intense. She never felt this way with any other guy—not even Sebastian.

She looked away suddenly, "Okay."

"Look at me, Tania," he demanded.

She obliged, "Why are you looking at me like that?"

"So, I can do this," he stated in all of his confidence as he leaned over to kiss her. His lips felt so soothing on hers as he began to plant soft and sensuous kisses all over her lips. As the kissing became intense, his tongue slid into her mouth, and they made out until the cars behind them started to beep over and over at them in frustration because he hadn't put his foot on the gas to proceed through the green light.

"Well, alright then," she said in shock at the intensity and urgency in the manner which Sincere was behaving. He came a long way from the guy who wouldn't even go as far to grab her butt, to the tricks he had up his sleeve today. She wasn't mad at him either. *About time he started to unleash that beast... too bad I'm on this walker, or it would be on! Oops, did I just think those impure thoughts about him right now? Lord, please forgive me, but my man is FINE! In the words of Kierra Sheard, 'Save me from myself'!*

Finally, they arrived at Mother Helen's home that she had left to Sincere's parents. He took her bags upstairs while she made her way over to the sofa to rest her legs.

"Is Mrs. Phillips home?" Tania asked out of curiosity. She wondered why Sincere seemed not to be bothered with bringing her to their home— it was bad enough that both her mother and Kamal knew she was going to stay with him for New Year's. She got along with both of his parents; however, she still was raised on the formalities of those who are not married should not be spending the night and all up in each other's houses like that until marriage.

"Nope, actually both her and my dad are playing in a Bridge tournament in Detroit." She didn't know why, but she was always intrigued with the "Motor City." Growing up learning about Motown, and all three car plants (Ford, Chrysler and General Motors) housed in Michigan...not to mention the Detroit Pistons...her mother used to have a crush on former player, Tayshaun Prince. She had run into him once at a Subway and told Tania that he was such a gentleman.

"Oh, okay," Tania replied letting out a sigh of relief.

"Besides, what do you think we were going to do here?" he asked while raising an eyebrow in suspicion.

"I wasn't thinking anything," Tania lied.

"Good, because I wouldn't take advantage of you, especially while you're down right now."

But I want you to take advantage of me, she thought to herself. "Why thank you, kind, Sir."

"Unless you want me to," he said with a devilish grin.

"Okay, where is my Sincere, and what have you done with him?"

He picked her up and began to carry her upstairs to the bathroom where the Louis Vuitton bags were. "Welcome to your 'Spoil my Sweet T' party where you're the guest of honor."

He sat her down on the counter while he proceeded to run her some bath water. He instructed her to look inside her bags from the Louis store where he got her a handbag with the matching Apple watch band, boots and lounge wear. He had already read her mind when he saw her pause at the outfit he bought her, "You don't need any underwear tonight, Tania, I wanna see your beautiful body since your cousin and my roommate will be there the entire time, you're up there with me."

Tania became excited but realized quickly that she still would need underwear for tomorrow—good thing her hair was getting braided in less than twelve hours because she didn't know what Sincere was up to, nor what was about to go down. "I need some for in the morning when you drop me back off at home."

"Look down in the bottom of the other bag, Tania," he stated nonchalantly.

Down at the bottom of the bag was another small Victoria Secret bag filled with body creams, shower gel, a poof and also a bra and panty set.

"I guessed your bra size, so I hope everything fits."

A big grin began to spread across Tania's face. "I can't believe you're doing all of this for me! For real, what has got into you, lately?"

"I told you I miss you, Tania...being apart from you makes me crave being in your presence."

Sincere got up from running the bathwater, walked over to the counter, and helped Tania get undressed, and then carried her back over to the tub. He proceeded to bathe her while giving her sensual kisses with every lather and wipe down. Tania couldn't take it, moaning in satisfaction.

"Okay, baby I'm gonna need for you to calm down for me. I'm trying to show restraint here," he laughed while playfully flicking her with soap suds.

"What planet exactly did you come from? I mean, really...who does this? There's probably grown men out here that don't do half of this stuff or maneuver the way you do."

"This is true; however, I study a lot and research what makes a woman happy and satisfied."

"So, how many women have you made this 'happy'?" Tania asked.

He chuckled, "I knew you'd ask me that...actually, only one woman before you and she was literally a woman when I was thirteen."

"What?!"

"Yeah, so technically she doesn't count," he insisted, smiling.

"When's the last time you had any contact with her?"

"Truthfully, about two years ago when she invited me to her 'Fabulous at Forty' party."

"Oh wow, she was grown, grown!" Tania exclaimed, still shocked.

"But enough about that woman, when I have my pretty young thing right here, and right now in this tub and her body looking so right." He then asked Alexa to play the best of James PJ Spraggins radio.

Lord, I know you provide ways of escape, but I don't want to escape this one! "I'm going to need for you to stop spoiling me now before you get me loose."

He laughed to himself again. "Trust me, Tania...I'm not about to do anything to defile you...I appreciate you," he then kissed her on the lips. "I appreciate your mind," he added as he kissed her on her forehead, "and I respect your body, as well as your soul...you're so incredible...perfect...priceless." He instructed her to let him help her up and out of the tub while he dried her off, and then carried her over to his bedroom where he lay her down gently on his bed.

Sincere applied some of the Cream Blends White Tea body oil to every nook and cranny of Tania's body while massaging her—focusing heavy on the areas in her hips and legs. "Does this feel good to you?"

"Yes, it does. Thank you so much, baby," she said as his fingers began to move in between her thighs to begin to play with her warm spot.

"I got you, Sweet 'T," he said as he kept his eyes closed taking in her responses to his touch and concentrating on the pants and pauses in her breathing. Sincere let his fingers talk to her until she begged for him to take her. He then proceeded to lower his face to officially write his name on his sweet spot. He traced it slowly and ever so carefully, accentuating every curve of each letter in his name until she exploded.

He didn't know what had gotten into him that made him go there with her, but he knew that he didn't want to penetrate her all the way. Tania was still a virgin, and he wanted to make sure that she stayed that way for more reasons than one: he didn't want to marry her tainted, he didn't want to create a chance for her to have a baby while they were both in school, and most importantly it was a sin. He knew that even going this far was questionable, however since he would propose to her before they went back to Philly with him, he didn't mind his actions too much. *Lord, I know I'm messing up. I'm gonna stop now. Please forgive me…*

He knew how to practice semen retention from his first year at Temple where the girls had gone crazy over the young, super fine freshman who was mad smart and could ball like Lebron in addition to the dribbling skills and moves as a point guard like Allen Iverson and fearless defense like Dennis Rodman. Especially once he crossed the burning sands and became a member of the elite Alpha Phi Alpha Fraternity, Incorporated at the end of the last semester.

Ever since he locked Tania down, and gave his life to Christ, he had cut off his whorish ways, and he prided himself on not ever pressuring or leading Tania into having sex with him on top of curving some of the baddest females on campus who wanted badly to take a ride on the Sincere Phillips train.

"This 'D' only belongs to you, and when the time is right, you will get it proper…just not now." He pointed at her sweet spot, "Now, that is all mine…promise me, Tania."

"I promise, Sincere. I love you."

"I love you, baby."

Sincere removed his clothing until the only thing he had on left were the Hanes boxer briefs that he wore that day. He then climbed behind Tania and proceeded to hold her until they both fell asleep.

****

Ondrea woke up during the wee hours of the night having to use the restroom. As she stumbled in soreness over to the bathroom in her hospital room, images of the bright red clumps of blood and tissue in the water from the jacuzzi tub began to replay in her mind.

As she finished using the restroom and stood in front of the mirror while washing her hands, she became overwhelmed with grief. Feelings of anger and sadness began to try and overtake her. *Lord, help me! Why?!* were the only words Ondrea seemed to be able to formulate in her thoughts.

Kamal overhearing the flushing of the toilet, and faint sniffles coming from the bathroom, rushed to Ondrea's side. "Hey now, Lady," he said as he gently wiped away the tears on her face and swooped her up in his arms.

"P-P—please pray for me!" She cried out as she could not pretend to be strong any longer.

Kamal began praying, and Ondrea began to sob uncontrollably. "Lord, in Your name, move as only You can! You said by Your stripes we are healed, and Lord we are coming to You in this hour knowing that Your strength is made perfect in our weakness. Lord, we need You like never before! Send Your comforter as only You can, in the capacity Ondrea needs, Lord God. We praise You in advance for lifting heavy burdens and mending broken hearts. We will forever give you the honor, the glory and the praise that is due only in Your precious son, Jesus' Name, Amen, and Amen!"

Chapter Seven

Tyrin lay in his bed awake, with the quiet storm radio blasting Carl Thomas' "Summer Rain," thinking of Bria. *Man, I really need my shorty,* was all he could think about. It had to be a reason that he had ran back into her last week. Confirmation of the baby girl led him to believe even further that it was destiny for them to be together. He hadn't prayed in years, but that morning he prayed that God would show Bria how big his heart was for her, and that his love for her was eternal. "Only God can give you a companion and only God can give you a friend," he had heard the late, Apostle William A. Lash III say in one of his sermons he had watched on tv a few years back. Tyrin didn't know why various messages and sermons had been coming to him lately—he wasn't the "church-going" type.

He had done too much, saw too much and had made it up in his mind that God couldn't love him like that because of all that he had done. Bria always told him if God could redeem her from a life of sin, then He could do the same for Tyrin. He wanted to believe that. He had also heard no man was supposed to be an island unto himself, but the only friend that he had was in fact, Bria. After Chance died, Tyrin had no friends. Bria was the keeper to all of his secrets, darkest moments, and his dreams.

He grabbed his phone and started texting: **"Hey Breeze, we need to talk when you get the opportunity...holla at me...always."** *Welp, here goes nothing,* he stated as Tyrin then pressed "Send."

****

Sebastian scrolled through Tania's IG posts, hoping she hadn't erased at least one of her pictures. Instead, he found a reel of her and Sincere in her Story section. *Look at this clown ass nigga...he ain't nobody for real though.* As he lay in bed thinking about how she looked at him when he grabbed her face in his hands while in his car, he knew deep down the love was still there.

****

Dearron opened the garage to let his brother Dane, inside. He had come from dropping Treasure back home with her mother with Jonoah fed, changed and perfectly intact.

"Thanks, bro for taking 'Noah with you and the family today. Bria really needed the break."

"It's no prob, baby bro," Dane replied back to his twin.

"Dude, you are only older than me by two minutes!" 'D retorted.

Dane chuckled, "You right, you right…so, how are ya'll doing, bro?"

"We're doing alright, just getting ready for this little girl to arrive."

"Oh wow, congrats! You know dealing with Treasure aka 'The Queen,' I'll have some tips and pointers for you as she gets older and sneakier by the minute."

"I hear you brother…well, let me put him down, check on my wife and finish my notes for tomorrow's sermon."

In the middle of turning around to walk back out through the garage, he suddenly turned around to face his brother. "I'm proud of you, Dearron…I mean, from us as kids cutting the fool and always chasing girls, I have to admit you have always been the more mature one out of the two of us. You accepting your call to preach…I'm just really proud of the man, father, and husband that you are, real talk."

Dearron was speechless to hear these words coming from his blood. Sometimes those close to you are the hardest to be a witness for. "To God be the glory, man…it's definitely not an easy task, but He makes it bearable."

"True that, true that…alright, 'D," Dane said as he left out.

God, I thank You for being my peace in the midst of the storm, for there is no failure in You. In two weeks, I will know whether or not I will be the father of the life growing inside my wife. Lord, you know my heart's desires and I trust the Will and plan that You have for all of our lives.

Chapter Eight

"God morning, Lady," Kamal greeted Ondrea as she opened her eyes Sunday morning.

"Morning, Kamal—what are you doing here? Service starts soon, don't you need to be at the church?"

Instantly he became upset to the point his nostrils began to flare. "I can't believe you'd think I would leave you in the hospital alone right now. Pastor Samuels is preaching today—plus, we don't know what time you'll be getting discharged later."

"You're right, I'm sorry babe..."

"No worries, Lady...look at you operating like a First Lady already...trying to make sure the church is still straight," he said as he kissed her on her forehead.

"Yeah, I do care, Kamal."

"Oh, before I forget Bria wants to talk to you when you feel like it. I told her I would have you contact her once we were home and situated."

"It's cool, I can talk to her now...I may not feel like dealing with or talking to anyone once we are back at the house."

"You're right, love...how are you feeling though?" He asked, growing concerned. Something wasn't feeling right, and she was too calm now. Kamal silently prayed that depression would not begin to attach itself to his wife. *Lord, keep her mind...keep my baby with a sound mind. I trust You, Lord that You know what You're doing and ask that You keep my wife in that same headspace.*

Kamal left out of Ondrea's hospital room to give her some privacy while she was on the phone, and to go grab a cup of hot chocolate. It stayed cold in those hospital rooms.

****

Bria hesitantly reached for her phone, she didn't know if Tyrin was trying to call since she ignored his text, but her mood quickly switched after seeing her best friend's number on the caller id. "Hey cow, are you feeling?"

"I'm good, cow" Ondrea lied.

"You sure, you know me…"

"I know, I know. I'm good for real…I just cannot believe I was pregnant all that time. I had no idea."

"I'm so sorry, friend. I don't mean to veer off the subject a bit, but did Kamal tell you that I talked to him yesterday?"

"He did…why, what's up?"

"Well, you know that preacher's convention he's planning to leave to go preach at on this weekend coming up. He had invited 'D to come with him…I was thinking you could come stay with me while they're gone…what do you say, cow? All-night Insecure and Power Universe marathons, Graeter's Dark Chocolate Brownie ice cream…you know how we do!" Bria said with excitement.

"You know what, that's not necessarily a bad idea," Ondrea said as she began to perk up on the inside. Even the book of Proverbs, I think Chapter seventeen and verse twenty-two even says laughter is like medicine."

"Yes ma'am! Say no more, friend…I'm gonna get your air mattress shipped here—you know the King Koil ones—I got you…that way you can sleep in the guest suite downstairs with me!"

"Okay, we just have to make sure we keep 'Noah up so he can sleep through the entire night now."

"I forgot to tell you, as of last week, he started doing that."

"Alright, now we just need him to keep that same energy while I'm there."

"Yes ma'am…we're speaking it, right now," Bria looked at the time and knew she had to log on to the Zoom live streaming service so she could catch her husband delivering the word. "Real quick, let's say a prayer before we hang up: Lord, I thank You for my friend and

the wisdom of her husband to get her to the hospital in time, along with guiding the surgeon's hands in her procedure and leaving her in good health. I ask that You continue to strengthen her body, her mind and most importantly her soul. What the enemy meant for bad, You sure turn everything around for the good, and give beauty for ashes and for that we thank and praise You. In Jesus' Name, Amen."

****

"My key text is coming out of Isiah 43:2- 'When thou passeth through the waters, I will be with thee, and through the rivers, they shall not overflow thee: when thou walkest through the fire, thou shall not be burned; neither shall the flame kindle upon thee…my subject is 'Something About the Name'."

Bria smiled listening as she watched her husband from her MacBook, preaching Sunday's sermon. It encouraged her to know that he had fought through his depressed state to stand behind the podium again and give God the glory by allowing himself to be used.

"Sometimes you have to remind yourself of who Jesus is when you're like that ship out in nothing but raging waters, high winds, and all hell is breaking loose. Ships don't sink because of the water around them, only when water gets inside of them through cracks or holes. Saints don't let the crack and holes of your trials and tribulations get inside and penetrate your soul! Hebrews 12:1 tells us to lay aside every weight and the sin that we do so easily…Don't let that heartbreak and heartache leave you bitter! Don't let that grief in and overtake you! The only way through the storm is Jesus! The only way we'll make it when we have to take cover is Jesus!"

Shouts all around the congregation erupted, as the Holy Spirit filled the sanctuary. Six souls gave their lives to Christ, and Bria couldn't be prouder and happier for her husband and the ministry.

****

"Can you run that Jehovah Jireh back one more time?" Tania asked Sincere on their way to Sunday service at her stepfather's church.

"You right, that song is fire," he said as he pressed replay.

As they rode to Jekalyn Carr's sounds putting them in the mood to praise the Lord, Tania couldn't help but think about her mother, what hospital she was in, and how was she doing.

Even though Kamal wasn't in attendance that morning, Pastor Samuels delivered the Word strong in power and demonstration of the Holy Ghost. They were glad that they attended the service and also the prayer she had received for a continued quick recovery and healing process. Tania wanted so badly to walk—drive—anything but be stuck on the walker.

Her phone rang, "Hello?"

"Hey Baby girl, I was calling to let you know the discharge nurse just left and said your mom will be free to come home in the next hour...she's drawing up the paperwork now...where are you?"

"Sincere and I are just now leaving church—"

"Sincere? Okay, what's going on with you two? I thought he wasn't coming into town until Friday?"

"He said that he wanted to spend Christmas down here with me before me and 'T come back with him to Philadelphia."

"Alright, I hope he knows he's not staying in our house, though...I don't play that—"

"I know, dad...sheesh!"

Praise God, she called me 'dad' again...I see You working, Lord. Kamal thought to himself, smiling. "Alright now, we'll be home soon, and hopefully you'll be there when she comes in."

"I'm definitely not going to miss that opportunity," Tania stated.

"Good. I'll see you then...Bye-bye."

Kamal knew the plan but was trying his hardest not to give off the impression that something was up. When Sincere called to give him and Ondrea the heads-up last month, while he was scheduled to preach in the convention, he made sure that he wasn't on the schedule Sunday, Christmas Eve, so that he could witness his daughter-in-love become engaged. He really hoped that Tania had dealt with her feelings surrounding Sebastian and could not shake the vibe that something was unsettled between the two of them. He didn't want any problems for her or Sincere, his future son-in law.

****

"Starting to feel some type of way...call me, Breeze."

Bria knew she needed to respond to Tyrin's text messages, as she did not want him to go searching for her: **"Hey, 'Rin...I will reach back out to you in a few days. I hope you understand."** She hit send. *I hope this will keep him at bay...I don't need any interruptions with me and 'D.*

The phone notification went off again. She proceeded to read his response: **"Yeah, aight."** *Gosh, he just has to make this so complicated!* The baby started to kick profusely and by the wave of nausea that started up coupled with the increasingly painful headache that was developing, this situation was making her blood pressure go up. Being home alone at the moment was not good for her in this state. *Put the phone down, Bria*

70

and protect your peace! To be honest, the only joy right now outside of Christ, was the fellowship she was looking forward to with Ondrea in a couple of days.

Chapter Nine

"**M**om!" shouted Tania as she moved as fast as she could on her walker into the house and into the living room where her mother sat while Kamal was fixing her some chamomile tea.

Ondrea wrapped her arms around her only daughter. "Hey, baby! I missed you—how are you doing, first and foremost?"

"No, mom…you know you're the priority here. I'm fine."

Just then, Kamal greeted Sincere in the only way Alpha men can. Who knew that "Ice" would translate into him becoming an "Ice Cold Brother," in Alpha Land when he received his bachelor's in Criminal Justice a few years back? *When God changes your name, it sure is for a better meaning.* Kamal was proud that Sincere chose the best frat—in his opinion. In addition to him giving his life to Christ earlier this year, he became even more confident that Sincere was the better choice for Tania.

"Hello, Mr. and Mrs. Davis," Sincere chimed in.

"Hello, Sincere. It's a pleasant surprise to see you back in town…when did you get here?"

"Just yesterday afternoon. I wanted to surprise everyone—mainly Tania," he said brandishing that killer smile that melted so many hearts. "But back to you though, respectfully Mrs. Davis. I understand you just got home from the hospital?"

"Unfortunately, yes, I did. I guess you can stay in the room since you're practically family now," Ondrea caught the look of warning that Kamal gave her. She had to remember the Christmas Eve surprise. "I found out that I was about three months pregnant and was having a miscarriage when I arrived in emergency. They had to do some type of procedure due to some kind of cyst rupturing, in addition to the baby dying from the poison."

"No!" Tania cried out as she became overwhelmed with sorrow. "I wanted to be a big sister."

"We will still try again for that, Baby girl…we just need to make sure our family unit is bonded a little more tightly, and I believe it'll happen for us. Everything in God's timing—always remember that" said Kamal as he gave Tania a big hug of comfort.

"It will be alright, baby," Ondrea added. "Don't worry, honey. We're going to try again real soon," she said while giving Kamal a look of concern for her daughter.

Thanks, I just need a minute," she replied as she sat down next to her mother on the sectional.

Sincere cleared his throat, "Anyone want a pick me up? I could pick up some Chef Vino's for everyone."

"Thanks, Sincere…that'll be nice," Ondrea replied.

"You know the regulars," Kamal added.

"You got it, Sir," Sincere returned before heading out to recharge and grab the food. *Lord, I'm trying to come to You more than just when I need something, but this You see, and I am coming to You on behalf of the need of my girl and her family at this time. I ask that You come into their home and heart and make it alright for them. Comfort them as only You can. In Jesus' Name, Amen.*

****

Both Monday and Tuesday, Tania was happy to have Sincere drop her off and bring her home from the crew's hangout sessions. She was grateful that he never tried to crowd her space, and that she was free to hang out with whomever—including, Sebastian. Sincere knew that there was no real competition, and that Sebastian could not compare in his treatment towards Tania. *It's all lust and no love with this dude* he had told himself.

Whenever Sebastian saw the black Range pull up, he would begin to seethe with anger as he was forced to watch another guy help her and she ride off with him. She was not with him anymore, and he had to find some solace in that.

It was Wednesday afternoon when she bumped into Sebastian in the hallway while they were at Wendy's, on the way to the restroom. "Hey, Tania," he said.

"Hey, Sebastian."

"Hey, it's been a minute since we've been alone in the same space...how have you been?"

Before she could answer the question, Londyn popped up. "Hey, Sissy, came to see if you needed any help...what are you two talking about?"

Tania rolled her eyes, "Nothing at all, I just bumped into him in the hallway."

"Yeah, sure," Bria said teasingly. "You know good and well you two were talking about the bomb food at Waffle House the other day!"

"That food was bussin," Sincere agreed.

"It was okay—"

"Classic Tania...you never like something if both me and Londyn say we do!" He said laughing.

"Boy stop!" Tania returned. "My waffle was cold," she said laughing.

"On a more serious note, how's Mom Dukes doing?"

"She's alright, I'll tell her you asked about her."

"Thanks so much. Again, on the real, I'm glad we got to hang out the other day

after your physical therapy. If you ever need another fill in anytime soon, just hit me up...seriously."

"I appreciate the gesture, however Sincere is in town, so he's gonna be my transportation until we go up to Philly next week—"

"You leaving town for what? I mean, seriously, what about your therapy or is he that selfish he only cares about him?"

"Seriously? The only reason you acting like you care now is because you know someone else is interested in and actually loves and cares about me the way I need to be cared for and loved on...don't hate on my man!"

Her man...The words hit Sebastian like a ton of bricks. Even Londyn fought back the urge to say, "*Dang!*" "That's what's up...I got the hint and I'll fall back. Hope he makes you happy, or I'm coming back for my spot." He walked off, leaving Tania speechless.

"Girl, you hear that?!" Londyn said in shock—mouth wide open. "He's coming for you, Sis!"

"I ain't going...girl, Sincere is my world. Do you know he gave me a full body massage and did not pressure me to have sex with him not even once? What guy does that anymore?"

"I don't even know one...not even your big-head cousin!"

"Right!" laughed Tania. "But, for real...things are so different with Sincere. I mean, he lives up to the meaning of his actual name. He's so gentle and genuine in his approach with me. I've never felt this safe and secure in my life. Even with my legs and hip all jacked up he has me not even the least bit insecure when it comes to that, Londy—it's like he's perfect."

"Yeah, a little too perfect."

"What you thinking, bestie? You think something's up with him?"

"I'm not saying all that, just be careful."

"You sure it's not because your bias with Sebastian?"

"Girl, my loyalty is to you...I want what makes you happy. I just don't want you to put all your trust in a man."

"Is all this coming from 'T coming up to Temple with us? Londyn, my cousin loves you and he's gonna have his groupie repellant on—trust!" she said as she side bumped Londyn, who was wearing a look of nervousness on her face.

"I hear you, Tania but we're all young..."

"Yeah, but he's not young and dumb. He knows he can mess up his family if he acts up. He knows you ain't going."

"I sure hope so."

****

Kamal said his goodbyes to his wife, Bria and his godson, Noah and met Dearron in the garage for a ride to the convention in South Carolina. Dearron began backing out of the driveway, looking forward to the strength of fellowship with his brother in Christ, and increasing faith through hearing and hearing more of the Word of God for the next couple of days.

"So, brother, did you handle your situation like I told you?"

"Man, situation was handled."

"That's what I'm talking about, bro," as they gave each other dap.

"However, I can't lie in saying that I'm over what she did."

"Honest question... if the baby isn't yours, do you think you can love her still and embrace the baby as if she was your own?"

"I honestly don't think so, and that's what scares me. I love Bria, God knows that I do...but that other part..."

"Yeah, brother, I am praying for you because I wouldn't want to have to deal with something like that. I mean, Tania is part of the package deal that I knew what I was signing up for."

"Exactly. I didn't sign up for all of this, bro."

"Well, I'm praying everything works out in your favor, seriously. I love you both and want God's perfect Will to be done in your lives. You'll have your confirmation soon."

"Thanks brother. So, what's new with you? How are you and 'Drea doing with what happened?"

"Honestly, I'm not okay. I really wanted that baby to still be growing—I'm not saying God can't do it again, but every time I've been feeling a certain kind of way about it, Ondrea is so sensitive and has been trying to fight off depression, that I have to hold it when it comes to my emotions. I have to exemplify strength for her, even when I'm falling apart."

It was now Dearron's turn to school his mentee. "Bro, you know that you have to cast your cares...you cannot carry all of that on your shoulders—God forbid."

"Naw, bro that's continuing in sin that grace may abound—"

"Right, and not giving it to God is trusting in yourself to handle it yourself...a pastor who does not trust God to handle it on His own? That sounds more like an oxymoron than the scripture being fulfilled in your life."

"That's why you're the GOAT in this thing, preacher!" exclaimed, Kamal in excitement and he pounded the dashboard. "You Uncle Willie's son!" he said in the best Mike Epps interpretation of "Day Day" from the movie, Next Friday.

"Brother, you are something else!" Dearron said laughing hysterically.

"Naw, I hear you, bro," Kamal returned. "Now, how much longer do we have until we get to Birmingham?"

Dearron looked on the Waze GPS calculator, "according to this, just a little over an hour before we arrive."

"Cool, then I can catch a couple of 'ZZ's' since your sis had me up talking all night." Kamal replied as he adjusted the seat in Dearron's 2022 Nissan Maxima.

"Naw, naw brother...wake up! You get no rest until death," he joked and turned on his Satellite radio. "Back To Eden" was playing.

"Oh, no! You gotta change that, brother...that gets no play in my ride."

"That's why we're in mine," Dearron chuckled as he began blasting one of his favorite songs by Donald Lawrence and the Tri-City Singers.

"Alright then, it's like that, bro?"

"Come on and live!" Dearron sang to the top of his lungs as he cruised on the highway towards their destination.

****

Ondrea looked down over Jonoah's bed as she watched him sleeping peacefully. She had just put him down for the night for Bria and couldn't help but stare at him, wondering if the baby she and

Kamal had just lost was a boy. *Lord, please allow me to be able to bear a child for my husband. We need a complete family, Lord. Please heal the hole in my soul. Deliver Me.*

"'Drea, come on let's get this party started...what we watching first?" Bria was already positioned on her Love sac with her Firestick in hand.

"Now you know I love me some 50 Cent, chile...Raising Kanan is where it's at!" Ondrea replied as she entered the living room from grabbing some spoons and the Graters's ice cream from the fridge.

"Awww, I wanna see my man, 'Lance,' by way of Jay Ellis!" Bria pouted.

"Girl, no wonder you're with 'D's square behind," Ondrea joked.

"Better a square than a real gangster!" Bria responded.

"Okay, okay you won that one…but correction, my man's delivered!"

"Praise God now let's get these marathons on the road," Bria said with much excitement. "You can pass me the other spoon and ice cream…we are eating out the carton like old times, I love it!" she added.

They must have stayed awake watching Power Book III: Raising Kanan for the first two seasons when Bria's phone went off for the fifth time. She looked at the text annoyed, and Ondrea knew who it must have been.

"So, Cow, what's up with that?"

Bria paused the show sighing, "Tyrin is not taking no for an answer. Ever since he found out the baby is a girl; he is more persistent than ever with me."

"Just like, Chance…well, it runs in their family."

"'Drea, I'm serious! I love Dearron, but I can't shake this man!"

"Okay, I'm gonna ask you a question and I'm going to need you to keep it real with me…do you 'love' Tyrin or 'in love' with him?"

Immediately, Bria began to think long and hard. "I honestly don't know, 'Drea."

"Well, Sis, that's what you need God to give you clarity on."

"That's just it—you think I've prayed that prayer?! I've prayed it over and over, and over again. I've loved 'D ever since we were seventeen."

"And truthfully, how long have you and Tyrin been messing around behind his back?"

"Off and on since I was seventeen," she admitted while dropping her head.

"No, hold your head up!" Ondrea said as she pushed her best friend's face up and helped wipe away the tears starting to trickle down her cheeks. "You've been avoiding this real question that you need to be honest with yourself and answer."

Bria thought about how many times she had been intimate with her own husband, but as good as he put it down, it still never reached her soul. It was then that she realized that she had never truly made love until the day Tyrin invited her over to "talk things out," and he had played the keyboard while singing Tank's "You Never Knew" to her. Things like that meant the world to her—the little things. He had a way of letting her into his personal world that no one knew about. The fact that he loved spoken word, R&B old school and 90s hits, not to mention that he could speak Spanish and Latin, read the dictionary, just didn't want others to know about it. True intimacy in having that safe and secure feeling with the person you are with.

"I love Dearron, but I wish he did everything and handled me like 'Rin."

Ondrea became uneasy for her friend, "Houston, we have a problem!" she said as she stated the obvious. Her sister was definitely entangled. She silently prayed for Bria right then and there—careful not to interject her opinions unto her friend. *Help my friend become free, Lord to be with who You designed her to be with. Help her to be honest with herself and most of all, her husband and Tyrin. Let love win. It is so and it is well with her soul, in Jesus' Name, Amen!*

****

"Sincere, you need to stop spoiling me so much," Tania told her boyfriend as he picked her up and carried her to the bench outside of her physical therapy appointment. She had laid eyes on yet another present he had bought for her since he arrived in town.

"Bae, its Christmas in two days, you know I was giving you your twelve presents up until that day...that's how I roll, so get used to this...like Lil' Flip said, 'I'll treat like milk, I'll do nothing but spoil you'!"

Tania busted out laughing as he then ran to go pull up his car, "you play too much!"

The more Sincere was around and they were vibing, her attachment to him became stronger and stronger. His presence was addicting. *Lord, help me to keep YOU first in our relationship. I don't want it to be a curse.*

Chapter Ten

"**O**uch!" Bria said feeling a bit of discomfort. She was starting to experience sudden sharp pains in her belly.

Ondrea immediately woke up, "What's wrong?!" she asked alarmed. She looked at the time...ten o'clock...she knew 'D and Kamal were probably already in a session. She didn't want to alarm them either if it ended up being a false alarm, but in case it wasn't who would they call for help? *Tyrin.*

****

"What's going on with Breeze?" he asked with urgency over the receiver. "Do I need to come on over there, or what...meet ya'll at the hospital? Let me know what's up, 'Drea."

"So...she's having some strong, sharp pains and I'm driving her straight to the hospital...do you need directions?"

"Memorial...she already let me read her birth plan at her last appointment, I'm ready."

Tyrin already had stuff packed for Bria and the baby in case of a situation like this. He knew Dearron was a popular Pastor in Georgia, and that it might be chance if Bria went into labor he may not be there. He had put two and two together and figured they must have worked things out and trying again by the way she had ghosted him.

Tyrin sped all the way in his Tesla to Memorial Health University Medical Center. Once inside the hospital, he found Ondrea in the waiting room.

They gave each other a quick hug, "Hey, family," he said affectionately.

"Hey, 'Rin…they are about to let us back to see her, they had to make sure everything was stable before determining if she was in active labor or not."

"So, is she?"

"Nope, just some hard contractions. This little girl is strong."

Tyrin stared at Ondrea with so much intensity, "That's my baby, 'Drea…I can feel it."

The crazy thing was that Ondrea actually believed him. She knew how adamant Chance had been about Tania. It's like they had a sixth sense or highly intuitive when it came to reading people—almost prophetic. She couldn't help but smile at the uncanny resemblance in demeanor and mindset. *Oh, Chance, you were something else, Sir.*

Just then, a nurse came out to lead both Ondrea and Tyrin back to see Bria. "She's in here resting right now, but we're going to keep her here overnight for observation in case her contractions pick up some more."

Jonoah started crying, and Ondrea picked him up to try and console him as he saw his mother laying in the hospital bed. "I'll stay with her," Tyrin stated matter-of-factly staring at the closed doorway to her room.

"'Rin…"

"I'll be good…promise, 'Drea."

"Alright, love you and tell my girl I got 'Noah."

****

Bria opened her eyes and found herself staring up at a white ceiling. *Why am I in here?* She touched her belly… *everything's still intact.* Her eyes then quickly glanced over at Tyrin sleeping peacefully on the couch bed in her room. *Why is he here?! Ondrea, that sneaky little…*

"What are you doing here 'Rin?"

"Well, good morning to you too, beautiful" he replied sarcastically.

"Tyrin…"

"Chill, Breeze, Ondrea called me because she wanted someone to stay here with you until they released you while she watched Jonoah…she knows I may be the dad, so it's only fair."

He had a point, but then again this was such an important event and again, here alone with her through it all was him. She smiled at him, "I guess you're right."

"Trust me, I'm not here to cause any trouble, Bria. I love you, but I love you more to fall all the way back. I got you always though…just know that alright…just want to make sure you and baby girl are A1."

"I love you too, Tyrin," she allowed her lips to say.

Alarmed, he immediately got up and came to her bedside. "Don't play with me, Breeze."

"I wish I was, 'Rin," she said as she looked up longingly in his eyes.

His eyes took in the emotions that had laid dormant deep in her soul for years. He returned the look with tears in his eyes, took her hand and kissed her on the back of it. "I've waited so long to hear you say those words to me…look at me, baby…"

Bria nodded in surrender to his command. "But what about Francesca?"

He rolled his eyes in disgust, "what about her? I'm not going to make you regret admitting that to me, baby. I'm gonna make this alright, trust. I actually prayed for this day."

"You can't hurt him. Dearron's a good man, 'Rin," she pleaded.

"I got all that, Breeze, but let me handle this for you. It's partly my fault you're in this mess. A real man doesn't have his woman out here looking bad."

Bria immediately regretted her admitting her horrible truth to her lover. She forgot who she was dealing with, and he was a man of honor, but at the same time, he wasn't afraid to take it there. All she could do in that moment was pray that when he left, that it wasn't to do any harm.

****

It was Friday, and the last day before Dearron and her hubby returned back to Georgia. As Ondrea packed some clothing to bring back to the hospital for Bria to change into before bringing her home, her phone began to ring. "Hey baby," she answered knowing it was Kamal.

"Hey baby, Dearron has been blowing up Bria's phone...everything alright?"

"Y-yeah," she stammered. "She's just been sleeping pretty heavy...she had a rough night, so she's resting. I took her phone so that she could do that, please tell him I'm sorry," she lied. *Lord, forgive me.*

"Alright, babe I'll tell him."

"How's the convention? You ready to tear the house down today?"

"It's been pretty good. I'm a little nervous, only because TD Jakes and John Gray are supposed to be on the panel at this morning's session, but other than that I've been fasting and praying in hopes that I decrease so that He can increase within me."

"I hear you baby, and I'm so proud of you."

"Yeah, Bishop Rainwater's wife said to tell you hello also," he added with a chuckle. He knew that his wife could not stand her, and had to rub it in.

"Hmph," Ondrea grumbled.

"Well, I love you and see you in the morning," he finished.

"I love you more."

"I love you deeper."

"No, you don't! When a woman loves, she loves for real!" she sang back in her best R. Kelly interpretation. They both laughed and then hung up the phone.

When she arrived at the hospital, Bria went hysterical as soon as she saw Ondrea.

"What's wrong?" she demanded. *I told him to be good!*

"I messed up and told Tyrin I loved him!" she said between sobs.

"Oh, honey," she said hugging her in a warm embrace, relieved that her friend finally came clean, but nervous for her and her future at the same time. "Lord, we thank You for providing the clarity needed in order for things to move forward as only you see fit. Help heal all hearts involved and protect this precious baby that still has to come into this world. Please forgive us of any sins committed knowingly and unknowingly and please continue to keep revealing those things that are sin we may not even realize we are committing. Should we continue in it that your grace stays with us—God, You forbid. In Your name, we pray…Amen and Amen!"

"Amen" Bria sniffled. She now had to face the music once and for all as soon as the baby came. That would be her way to settle all confusion.

Chapter Eleven

Kamal and Dearron made great timing on their ride back to their wives from Alabama. By 6:00 PM Dearron's car was parked back into his garage and he had entered into their first-floor guest suite to check on Bria. He found her resting.

"Hey bro, she's been really tired these last couple of days," Ondrea said to him as bent down to pick up Jonoah who had got off of his toddler tricycle to run over to his father.

"Hey man!" He exclaimed as he picked him up and gave him a huge hug. "Thanks for keeping an eye on her, Sis."

"Anytime. How did my man do this weekend?"

"He killed the convention…"

"To God be the glory, I cannot take any credit, bro…you know that," Kamal stated while extending his arms towards his wife to greet her with a hug and kiss.

"Aww, he's modest. You know your husband isn't going to tell you that both Pastor John Gray and Pastor Steven Furtick invited him to speak at their churches when he gets a chance. I'm telling you, I'm godly jealous."

"Hey, the student is never greater than the teacher, bro," Kamal said as he returned the compliment.

"Baby, that's amazing!" Ondrea said squeezing her husband tighter, as they kissed.

"You two save that for when you get back home!" Dearron joked with the two of them.

"Bro, we are crashing at your spot tonight before heading back…what you thought!" Kamal returned with a mischievous look.

"You know ya'll are more than welcome but do us a favor and throw the sheets in the washer on your way out tomorrow," he said laughing hard.

"Whatever, 'D! I'll call Tania and let her know to expect us home tomorrow." Ondrea called out as she left out of the kitchen to go back to watching tv.

****

Sincere had created the perfect impromptu date during the day, where they picked out the first book in the Ashley Antoinette series, Butterfly to read together and discuss. They were in there since earlier that morning.

"Hello?" Tania answered her cell as she and Sincere just finished leaving from the reading corner at Barnes & Noble.

"Hey Sweetie, what are you doing?"

"Sincere and I are leaving from Barnes and Nobles and about to grab something to eat before he drops me off at Bria's...she wanted to hang with me some before you came back home."

"Well, I was calling to let you know that Kamal and I won't be back until tomorrow now."

Tania looked at Sincere with a big smile, "Yes ma'am."

"Are you okay? How'd therapy go yesterday?"

"It went great. Dr. Washington said I am making great progress and they may perform my surgery before April, God-willing."

"That's great news, honey. I'll make sure I let your god mommy know all about her 'Taniecey-pooh'."

"Mom!' Tania replied with embarrassment.

"Girl, you know you will always be our baby no matter how old you get."

"I know, I know," she lamented. "What are ya'll about to do?"

"I don't know. With your godmother being on strict bedrest, we were thinking of either Door Dashing something, or Kamal and 'D grabbing us a carryout somewhere."

"Oh, alright…well, we're about to head into Keedra's Kitchen so I'll call you back…"

"It's alright, I'll just see you at the house tomorrow. Let me know if you need anything."

"Yes ma'am," Tania answered as she hung up the phone. She turned her head back to Sincere, "So, you never told me about our arrangements up at Temple…"

Sincere smirked, "You already know you have my bed. 'T will have my roommate's bed since he's going to stay in his girl's dorm while ya'll are with me. I will sleep on the floor next to you—I already know what you're thinking, and the bed isn't big enough for the both of us," he added as he saw the pouting she displayed on her face.

"I guess…well, what about New Year's Eve…what are we doing?"

"Well, I'm gonna hoop with 'T and let him meet the team early that morning, then when we're finished, I'm gonna take you guys to breakfast, shopping and then there is a lot of activities on campus…I figured we'd hit up the probate followed by step show, and there's an All-white party that night where we can ring in the New Year—as long as I get to kiss on you, I'm good," he said with his charming smile.

"You sure you want to show me off with this," Tania said as her countenance slowly started to fade as she looked down at her walker.

"Chill with that, Tania…you know I have never, and will never be ashamed of you. Your beauty is unmatched and you're so incredible—I told you that. I need you to believe it. The 'Tania Williams' that I know would let her confidence reign so supreme that after being in everyone's presence, she left them wondering how they could be down with her and her movement…Baby, you're a trendsetter, you're creative and have your own lane. You're so darn sexy that it makes no sense. Believe me, baby…I want you to," he said as he wiped tears from her face and held her close.

"I hate that I'm like this!"

"And it's only temporary, Tania. Remember that…you are getting stronger every day and that should let you how much of a fighter you are. The end is near," he continued speaking life into his girlfriend.

Sincere always knew what to speak into her to build her up. "I love you, Sincere," she said looking up into his eyes.

"I love you, Tania." He escorted Tania and her walker to the bench outside of the restaurant and ran to go to park his car.

****

Bria got a notification on her Apple watch that she had a missed call from Tyrin. She wanted to return the phone call, but Dearron was back home, and she didn't want to risk him, Kamal or even Ondrea overhear her conversation on the phone when she was supposed to be resting still. She decided to text him instead. **"Hey 'Superman,' just wanted to let you know I made it back home safe. About earlier, if you truly love me…it never happened."**

Tyrin frowned in disappointment as he responded back to her. **"Come on now, you know I can't do that, Breeze. I lost you once because I didn't step up and lay claim to you like I should have, but I'm not about to let that happen again. This bed I'm laying in is supposed to have you in it lying next to me. These fingers I'm using to text you back should only be for touching you and these words I say are meant for me to be saying them to you face-to-face while we make love."** *I need for dude to be a nonfactor. That's my woman. MINE!*

Bria read Tyrin's response and was speechless. She had no comeback. She knew he was telling the truth.

Chapter Twelve

Christmas Day was finally here, and the Davis household couldn't be more filled with joy and peace than now. Donny Hathaway's "This Christmas" was blasting through the house, and the smells of soul food and her mother's famous Sweet Potato souffle' filled the house.

"Hurry up, Baby girl, your mom's in here about to get hangry," Kamal teased as he called upstairs.

"Almost ready, dad!" she yelled back. Tania was trying to get herself cute for the Christmas family pictures her mom told her they were going to institute every year, starting today. She was comfy and cute in an oversized red knitted Gucci pullover sweater, with black leggings and matching red Uggs. She hated that she couldn't wear her heels yet, but she would take Sincere's advice and still slay like the diva she was. She applied some Benefit lip glass, flipped her microbraids to one side, and couldn't help but smile at the results in the mirror that looked back at her. She was a natural beauty and couldn't be more thankful to God for Him giving her the looks that He did.

Both Ondrea and Kamal looked astonishing in their matching tan and red colors—Ondrea in a red Gucci sweaterdress and black heels, and Kamal in red and black Gucci cardigan, black shirt, and black slacks with the matching monogrammed Gucci loafers.

As Tania and her walker made the way down to the top of the staircase, she was confused as to why the music changed from Christmas music to Jesse Powell's "You."

"Hey!" she called out, mad that they changed the song.

"Just you and your walker get down here, now!" Ondrea's excitement began to build up even the more.

Tania made it all the way to the bottom of the stairs, and as soon as she turned the corner, there was Sincere in all black with a matching Gucci belt and loafers like Kamal on his knees searching for something under the entryway table in the foyer.

"Sincere, what you looking for? I'll help…" Tania asked sincerely.

Instantly, he sprang up on one of his knees with what appeared from his back pocket a Zales ring box. He opened up the box to display the 2-carat princess-cut diamond ring he had bought her before.

Immediately her eyes became wet with tears of happiness and surprise. "No way!" she squealed.

"Go ahead and pinch me baby, its real," he said as he took her hand. "Tania Paige Willliams, I loved you ever since I met you at my Grandmother Helen's church. I still remember your outfit, they way you wore your hair, and even your perfume scent you had. You are a breath of fresh air to me. I thank God every moment for giving me the love of my life—a young woman who is not only intelligent and saved, but secure within herself and sexy as all get out—no disrespect Mr. and Mrs. Davis," he said with a chuckle.

"Watch yourself!" Kamal said as they all laughed. Kamal and Sincere performed their ritual greeting handshake in approval to move forward in his proposal.

He then turned his attention and focus back to Tania. "No, but seriously, my Sweet T, you would make any man blessed to call you their wife, and I'm hoping that you'd make that fantasy a reality for me…will you marry me, Tania?"

He took her hand again while looking up into her eyes and placed the ring on her finger. She covered her mouth in disbelief that this moment was happening in her life at this precise time. "Yes, Sincere….AHHHHHH!!!!" she cried out in sheer bliss.

93

Sincere got up off the floor and gave her a quick kiss on her lips and then forehead. Although he wanted to give her a longer kiss and hug her tighter than he did, he wanted to make sure that he was respectful of their daughter—especially while in their home and was careful in how he spoke to and handled Tania during his visit.

****

When everyone retired for bed, Tania turned on her music player to Kelly Price's "He Proposed." She had it set to play on repeat. Then it dawned on her...*I need to tell Londyn!*

"Merry Christmas, Sissy!"

"Merry Christmas," Tania replied.

"Merry Christmas, Cuz!" Tyrin Jr. yelled in the phone.

"Sshhh, why are you screaming, 'T!" Londyn snapped.

"Whatever, babe. Facetime Tania right now and show her your present." he demanded.

"You don't tell me what to do, homie!"

"Who are you talking to? You talking to a man right here...come on, show her!"

Londyn switched her call to Facetime where as soon as they saw Tania's face pop on the screen, 'T held up Londyn's hand displaying the massive rock on her ring finger.

"Shut up?!" Tania responded in shock.

A huge smile began to spread across Londyn's face in confirmation, and she nodded her head, 'yes'.

"Congratulation's you guys! I am so happy for you two...see, I told you Londy—"

"Yeah, you did...so, how was your Christmas?"

She couldn't hide it any longer and pretended to wipe her eye with her ring finger, displaying her ring as well.

"Bihh! You're lying!" Londyn exclaimed.

"Yooooo.... that ring is aight though," 'T stated.

"Double wedding, heffa!!!! Who proposed, though?" Londyn asked in curiosity.

"Don't do that! It's not obvious?"

Both Londyn and 'T looked at each other, and then back at Tania, "No."

Instantly, Tania became upset. "How is it not obvious?"

"Chill out, cuzzo...it's just you got two dudes on you heavy at the same time."

"Ha, ha...very funny. In case you really cared, Sincere asked me."

"Girl, I knew he was going to ask you sooner or later."

"How did you know? How long did you know?"

"Girl, since before your mother's birthday...he had me help pick your ring out on Facetime since I was pretty much due with Journey at that point."

"Oh wow..."

"Well, I'm happy for you either way, I meant that," Londyn told her friend.

"I'm cool with it also, Tania. I don't have no problems with Sincere, and I believe his intentions is honest with you."

"You're sure you're not just saying that so you can be guaranteed a spot on Temple's team when we graduate?"

"I see you got jokes," 'T returned. "Naw, I really fool with the cat the long way, pause, but on some real ish, I can tell he love you for real."

Tania smiled at her cousin's response. She never told him, but 'T's opinion meant so much to her. He and Tyrin Sr. were her protectors for the many years that she did not have a father figure in her life to do so.

"Thanks again, 'T…that means a lot to me whether you know it or not."

"I know even though we are cousins, we were raised up like brother and sister. I'm gonna always have your best interest. The best man apparently won…where's he at? How come ya'll ain't up celebrating?"

"You know Kamal ain't going, 'T," she laughed to herself.

"Damn, I mean ya'll are engaged now…"

"Yeah, but we aren't married yet."

"How much trouble he think ya'll gonna get into though, I mean you walking around on a walker, for real, for real."

"You'd be surprised…"

"Awww, hell naw…I don't wanna hear that!" 'T exclaimed getting out of the camera.

Londyn was cracking up laughing, "ya'll nasty!"

"Says the one with a baby," Tania shot back.

"Touche,' Heffa!" Bria retorted.

"Love you guys, I'm starting to get sleepy."

"Umm hmmm, I bet…love you too,"

"Bye."

****

Ondrea finished putting on her night gown and watched as Kamal undressed and put his pajama bottoms on as she lay across their

California King-sized bed. They had just finished enjoying a nice and steamy shower together and the mood was set for rest and relaxation. She admired how much he took care of his body, and even more she loved looking at his dark chocolate, flawless skin. He was perfect to her in every way. She thanked God that he has been her rock through all of the ups and downs she has faced since she met him. He truly was her blessing that came from a curse.

"Babe, can you believe Tania is engaged? We actually let him do this?"

"Now 'Drea, remember I told you when he came to us that they won't actually go through with a wedding right now. She still has to graduate high school—"

"That's just it, Kamal… her and 'T found out that they can graduate early due to the amount of credits they have, exam scores and their SAT/ACT scores."

Kamal didn't prepare himself for that scenario. He prided himself for always being three steps ahead of the game. *Man, I'm slipping.* "Ondrea, how come you didn't let me know when this happened?"

"Babe, I'm sorry, I thought she told you when she came home from school that day…it was towards the beginning of the school year. I talked to Grace, and she said 'T also proposed to Londyn today…Lord, these kids and the love they think they know they are in."

"That's just it, 'Drea…they don't know nothing about real love."

"Like what we have," she said smiling at him as she started massaging his neck, shoulders, and back. She knew he was steaming mad and wanted to calm him down. She noticed Kamal did have a little trouble with his temper if he wasn't prayed up.

"Yeah, babe…you know, maybe I should have a class with our young people on relationships and marriage next week."

"That's a great idea. You can announce it at bible study Tuesday."

"Thank you, Lady…that's why my First and Only Lady is the woman I'm on this bed with right now," he said turning around to look her in the eyes. *My baby is so beautiful. Thank You, Lord for my good thing. I definitely have obtained favor.*

"Is that right?" Ondrea said flirtatiously.

"Woman don't play with me," Kamal returned while biting his bottom lip.

"Or what?" she returned as he changed positions in the bed to show her exactly what he meant.

Chapter Thirteen

"What's up 'T?" Sebastian said as he greeted his friend after their basketball game. Their team ended up beating the home team by twenty-six points, and both young men had impressive numbers in rebounds, assists and overall points during the game.

"Hey, you got a sec, I need to holla at you about something that happened yesterday."

Sebastian braced himself. "What's going on?" He instantly thought something happened to Tania. "Is it Tania, she alright?"

"Yeah, she's alright, but engaged now."

Sebastian looked stunned.

"I know, bruh. I owed it to you to give you the heads up though. Sincere asked her yesterday."

Those words landed like a ton of bricks to his chest. "Damn, bruh...I lost her for real...man, I messed up bad."

"Dude, they just got a vibe that's all. She seem really happy with him and he do love her though, bruh—on some real shit."

"I'm not denying that."

"Then you got to accept that. Yeah, you messed up, but at this point you want to make sure you two don't lose the friendship you have. Trust me, if you really love her, you'll want to always be there in good times and bad. Always make sure you're available because love isn't about your pride."

"Listen to you spitting some real ish like you an old man."

"I'm just trying to put you up on game. Londyn is a different breed so I had to learn how to maneuver with her, and cuz is cut from the same cloth…if they meant to be, it will be and if not, then let her go bruh. For real, if she is then she'll come right back," Tyrin said as he dapped his best friend up.

"Good looking," Sebastian replied.

Chapter Fourteen

The flight was not long at all, and they were very accommodating of Tania and her walker. She was able to use a wheelchair while getting around in the airport.

'T was anxious to see what would await him at one of his prospective schools. The advantage was that he already knew Sincere—who was one of the nation's most sought-after college basketball player. From the many games they played, 'T was able to pick up on a lot of technique and ball-handling skills usually reserved for the big leagues.

Once they arrived on the campus, both Tania and 'T received quite their fair share of stares—and for very different reasons. On one hand, Tania was very beautiful and had the best physical features, however with her on a walker, some of the players and women on campus could not grasp their minds around the female Sincere had been bragging about and being faithful for. For the women who saw 'T—again, like his father, lust was always in the eyes of a female who was drawn in by their overwhelming attractive features—not to mention 'T's baby blues.

As they carried Tania and their suitcases while entering the building that Sincere's dorm was located, 'T couldn't help but lock eyes with the brown-skin cutie with the stylish pixie cut, coming out the entryway. She purposely bumped her rear end into him as soon as his first leg stepped inside the hallway, "Oops, I'm so sorry, cutie!" she said, slyly while winking her eye at him.

"I-It's okay," he stammered, stunned by her beauty and forwardness. One thing that was a turn on for 'T was an assertive woman. *Oh Jesus, if the women are like this on a college campus, then I'm in trouble,* He admitted to himself. He made a promise to himself not to look her way again for the rest of the weekend if she reappeared. *Man, Londyn will have to live with me for sure up here!*

****

Saturday morning, Sincere introduced Tyrin to his basketball squad as they all played a quick pick-up game. Some of the teammates told 'T that they would love to have him on Temple's team if and when he decided to come out of high school and graduate. Sincere had already let them know he was eligible to graduate early, and that he was serious about basketball.

"Yeah bruh, once you come here you can start accepting endorsements and we also get paid for our team and characters being featured in the college video games.

'T's eyes widened in surprise, "You bullshitting?"

"Nope," Sincere confirmed. "That Range was part of the money I got from being a star in the video game, and I may have an endorsement with Distinct Life, bruh! That's big news…I've even been approached about entering the draft this year."

"Hold up, fam—you only in sophomore year, right?"

"Yep, but the stats and boards I'm putting up, puts me in the first round in the top five of picks."

"Good shit! Dang, man Cuz might trip though if you leave her."

"I'm gonna try and get her to come with me if I go to a team."

"Good luck with that one, fam…you know your girl is stubborn."

"Facts," he agreed as they both chuckled.

"Yours is too, and she'll cut you if you get caught up with any of these females here."

"…And that's also facts! My dude, I'm gonna have to buy some brown contacts or something to hide these eyes…they get me attention I don't even want."

102

"Especially when you become a starting player on the team, bruh!" Sincere warned. "These chicks are like hounds. You know how they say the enemy is like a roaring lion, seeking whom he may devour?"

Tyrin stood looking clueless.

"You never been to church, or heard that scripture, John 10:10, fam?"

"Naw, my dad wasn't really into us going to church like that…" Tyrin said feeling a little embarrassed by how little he knew about the Bible or God. Londyn had tried various times to get him to attend church with her. When he found out Kamal was a minister there, that made it even more hard for him to go and receive any Word, when the very man who was giving the Word killed his older cousin back in the day.

"Well, the devil sends all kinds of females to tempt you to throw you off your game, and even get pregnant by you because you're their ticket out their hood or ticket out of college early…bottom line, just beware of the booty," he said laughing.

"So, I know you weren't with my cousin the first part of your freshman year…how difficult for you was it?"

"Man let's just say threesomes, foursomes, fivesomes—you name it, I went hard. Definitely some of these jawns been passed around for sure. Good thing we found our Queens early, because these other dudes here have a slim pick."

"Who's the ones that you think are acceptable on campus?"

"Why you wanna know is the bigger question, fam?" Sincere picked up what was happening.

"Just curious…" 'T said nervously.

"Curiosity killed the cat…kind of like, D'auria," he said while looking over at the girl who had bumped 'T in the entryway hallway warming up with the rest of the cheerleaders.

'T shook himself, "A freaking cheerleader...Fam, she was on me heavy!"

"Yeah, she's a jawn for real...there's a lot you gotta be schooled on, fam—not just on the court, I see."

"Man, dude whatever...thanks."

"Alright, now let's get back before I hear it from your cousin," Sincere joked.

****

"'D, I think this is it!" Bria yelled out. She was experiencing very sharp pains that were happening now at a fast and alarming rate.

Dearron ran downstairs to come to the aid of his wife who he found sitting on the toilet rocking back and forth in agony. "Hold on honey, I'm about to get you to the hospital...which one do you go to?" he asked as he fumbled trying to get his phone out of his pant pocket.

"Memorial..." she struggled to get the word out.

"Okay," he said. He then called Dane to see if he or his wife could meet him at the hospital and grab Jonoah while he with Bria.

"Hurry!" she called out in pain. Bria tried desperately to remember how to breathe through her contractions—which were now coming harder, faster with each one stronger than the last.

Dearron hurried to strap Jonoah in his car seat, lay the towels down in the car, and proceeded to speed all the way to the hospital. Once inside and situated, Bria mustered up enough strength to ask Dearron to contact Ondrea and also Tyrin. *I'll call Ondrea, but that nigga can go to Hell for all I care! This is a special moment for my wife and I...I don't need any outsiders.*

"Hello?" answered Ondrea. She looked at the time on her iPhone. 10:18 PM.

"'Drea, it's 'D…Bria is in labor right now."

Ondrea sat straight up in the bed stirring Kamal as he had been sleeping peacefully like a baby. "Okay, I'll be right there!"

"What's going on, babe," Kamal asked in a groggy voice while trying to wake up. He knew it was late, so an emergency was imminent.

"Bria is in labor, right now!"

"Say less, let's get you to your friend," he said as he threw off the covers up off of him, jumped up and put some clothes on.

****

They are probably gonna kill me for this, but he needs to know, Ondrea thought to herself as she proceeded to call Tyrin to let him know what was going on.

"Thanks, 'Drea, I appreciate you calling. I knew he wasn't going to. I'm on my way—"

"Hey, Tyrin," Kamal interrupted. "I hope you don't get offended, but right now, I think it's wise to just make sure that you're in position, but let's get her through a stress-free and healthy delivery first."

As upset as it made him to hear this, Tyrin knew Kamal was correct in his thought process. "Alright, I'm trusting you two to let me know every detail in how Bria is doing and how the delivery goes," he said with great concern.

"We got you, 'Rin," Ondrea assured him before hanging up from the Bluetooth in the car. Kamal sped so fast to the hospital because if Tyrin was anyone that thought like him, if he hadn't heard anything by a certain time, he meant business, and coming up there anyway.

Tyrin sat on the couch with his head in his hands. *Damn, I mean, Darn…Sorry, Lord, forgive me for cussing. I'm not that good at these prayers but asking that you help calm my nerves and help me stay patient until I hear more from Ondrea or her husband. In Jesus' Name.*

****

"Girl, You two are killing 'em!" Londyn exclaimed as Tania modeled her all-white, ruffle-sleeved bodycon dress and gold accessories for the Temple's New Year's Eve All-White party thrown by the black Greek organizations on campus.

Sincere was matching her in an all-white suit with gold pocket square. "Why thanks for the compliment, family," he said sneaking up behind Tania, holding onto her from behind and kissed her on the cheek.

"Ugh, I don't want to see all that...where's my fiancé'?" Londyn asked.

"I'm getting dressed still, babe!" he hollered from inside Sincere's bathroom in his dorm. When he emerged from the bathroom, he was rocking an all-white Levi jean outfit with the matching jacket. His Wallabee boots, and LV belt for accessories matched his baby blue eyes.

Londyn took one look at him and became very insecure. "You look good, Tyrin...don't forget about home though."

'T cut his eyes at her sternly, and sighed, "Who's finger did I put a ring on?"

"Mine," she said proudly holding it up in the camera.

"Exactly...I remember, but don't you to start tripping and forget," he told her, slightly annoyed.

"Okay, I guess you're right."

"Trust me, Londyn. Nobody is holding my attention like that," 'T said while he was remembering the D'auria, freshman baddie that tried him in the hallway yesterday.

"Holding your attention like that?" Londyn replied back with a scowl on her face.

"You reaching now…I love you, we'll check back in," he returned with reassurance in her spot being secured.

"Okay, 'T,'" she said with a little more confidence, but still couldn't shake the feeling that something wasn't right up there. Just then, sounds of Journey starting to cry were heard from the baby monitor.

"We love you, Londyn!" Tania yelled in the phone before ending their Facetime.

****

Dearron met both Ondrea and Kamal at the front entrance of the hospital. He was wearing a sullen and somber look that immediately had the two worried.

"Wh-what's wrong?!" Ondrea asked as she braced herself for the worst.

Tears welled up again in Dearron's eyes, "Both Bria and the baby's heart rates dropped, and Bria is in intensive care in an induced coma, and the baby is d-dead!" he mentioned to get the words out before punching the wall outside.

"No!" screamed Ondrea, as Kamal caught her before she hit the ground.

Some moments later inside the conference room, sat the three of them. After the doctors confirmed the baby girl's blood type was O and Bria's is BO—which meant Dearron was not the father because his was AB negative. The other parent's blood type in order to make an O baby had to also be BO…All were in shock.

Finally, Kamal broke the silence. "So, who's going to make the call to Tyrin?"

"Dude, you can't be serious right now!" Dearron fumed. "I just lost the baby I was hoping was mine, and my wife is fighting for her life, and you wanna call this nigga in?!"

Kamal's nostrils began to flare, but he had to remind himself that his friend was hurting. "Bro, you of all people know I don't want to have to contact him either. But look at me, 'D...we are The Lord's manservants, first and we have to do what thus says the Lord. We know now the ugly truth—and it's ugly, bro...we have to keep it real, but he lost his baby girl tonight."

Silence fell in the room.

"So, I need you to pray and ask God to allow peace to prevail while your wife is in there fighting for her life. When she comes out of this—and I said when, she is going to need all of us to get through. If you love her, bro do that for nobody but her."

He nodded yes in defeat. "Alright, but when he gets here, I don't want to look at him. I honestly can't promise to practice temperance, meekness, joy, patience, or long-suffering...none of that right now, bro!"

"Understandable, you can be angry, but sin not and let no sun go down on your wrath."

"Well, pray for me that the Lord has mercy on my soul, brother because this ain't a quick bounce-back.... we are talking about my wife smashing that street nigga behind my back, getting pregnant and giving birth to his fucking baby on top of all of that...man fuck him!

Kamal immediately hugged his brother in the gospel with force and went into straight prayer mode. "I'm praying for you angels to come and minister to your manservant who needs ministering to. I loose peace for my brother, Dearron. Lord God, I said peace right now to my brother!" Kamal hugged him tighter. "Calm his spirit right now, in Jesus' Name!" Kamal said with power and authority.

Once Kamal's prayer of deliverance cleared his conscience, Dearron then returned to visit Bria in her room before heading to Dane's to cool off.

Chapter Fifteen

*G**od, I thought you said if I come to You humbly, You'd hear my prayers. If this is punishment because of us sinning, then Lord, You could've taken me and not my baby girl. Bria don't deserve none of this. God, she has been through too much. I know I was moving foul, Lord but she really was confused. I don't know if I am sent by the devil to her or if You really made her for me, but I'll back all the way up if You allow her to live. I love her that much, God. You took my daughter, but Lord, don't take, Bria.*

Tyrin had just hung up with Kamal who delivered the devastating news. Ondrea was too outdone emotionally to even have words to put in sentences. Kamal waited at the entrance for Tyrin.

"Aye man, I'm telling you now, I'm gonna need one of those magic prayers you do, Kamal. I can't lose her."

In that moment, he hated to admit it, but God showed him Tyrin's heart for Bria. Genuine love, care, and concern. Not out of selfish greed, but from a pure and unconditional reserve. It was a familiar spirit of love he picked up due to the fact that it was identical to how he was when it came to Ondrea…a Godly, Agape love.

"Trust me, Kamal I have prayed over Bria. I want to give you my condolences for the loss of your daughter with her. I know she shared that you knew it was a girl from the beginning and that she was yours."

"Thanks, man. I mean I have feelings and thoughts a lot of the time that come true."

"So, you flow in the prophetic?"

"The who?" he asked sincerely.

"I'll make sure we talk after all this is over, Tyrin."

"Alright, then...will they let me back to see her or the baby?"

"You still want to see the baby?" Ondrea asked.

"Of course, that was my little girl...I'm going to see her first before they take her in case Breeze doesn't wake up in enough time."

Tyrin then went up to the nurse's station to inquire about seeing his deceased baby. Once they brought him to the postmortem area, he laid eyes on his baby girl. He immediately felt something come over him that led him to pick her up as if she was alive and began to pray over her.

"Daddy's here, baby girl. Daddy and Mommy were waiting for you...you're so pretty like your Momma. She's fighting for her life right now, and I need for you to wake up, baby. Wake up, baby girl. Do you hear me, Lil' One?" he commanded through the sobs. "This is your Daddy talking to you..." he kept talking to her as he felt her cold skin start to develop some warmth. *I don't know what's going on, Lord but keep and preserve my baby girl. She is precious and one of Yours.* As soon as Tyrin could say, "Amen," his baby girl opened her mouth and yawned.

"Nurse! Nurse! Somebody help! My baby is alive! Thank You, Jesus!" Tyrin almost dropped her while he was shouting for help and praising God all at the same time. *Can't nobody tell me You ain't real. You perform miracles, and I know you did when you allowed me to live. The same raising power You used on this ole' dressed up dirt, is the same power worthy to be used on someone as pure as my baby girl.*

Chapter Sixteen

During the month of February, Tania learned that she had come a lot further in her recovery than expected, and her final hurdle—surgery, was approved to be moved to the middle of March. This caused a small issue between her and Sincere due to her having both her surgery and recovery process during March Madness—the most important time in his life—there was no way she could come against this moment for him, and at the same time as much as Sincere didn't want to "leave her hanging," he had no choice in the matter if he cared about his future and the provision that would come for ways to be made in his basketball career—whatever that may look like.

Tania tried adamantly to persuade Sincere to finish his degree before pursuing an NBA career. She didn't understand the importance of him utilizing his young-adult years right now, while he was in his prime. Sincere promised her that he would take her into consideration now that they were engaged. This caused a lot of strain on their relationship because she knew basketball was his passion, and while she had the opportunity to graduate early at the end of this school year, she didn't want to if Sincere was not at Temple. That had been her plan all along, and this draft was messing that up for her.

They learned in the couple's class Kamal taught in church, that a lot is to be considered when you decide to take the next step into marriage. You not only have to be equally yoked spiritually, but a lot of the things that break up even the most saved individuals who were married for some time were the big three: sex, communication and money.

If they were going to make it as a young couple, they needed to remember that they needed to communicate more than having sex and be open and honest about their finances. Sincere did not like Tania questioning him about his spending and where he got his money from. He believed that she should automatically trust him when he told her what was going on because he would be the head. According to Tania, that was not so and that she had a right to know his dealings because she either could be directly or indirectly affected because of her attachment to him as a fiancée; and later on, his wife.

****

Londyn was so glad that 'T came to the class with them. He asked a lot of questions, and finally opened up to Kamal about his desire to learn how to be a good leader of his family, be dedicated to Londyn and controlling lustful desires. Kamal advised him that if he stayed coming and hearing The Word, studying on His own, as well as getting some spiritual counsel before and after they become married, he will be a successful man of God. 'T gave his life to Christ at that class and had over the last couple of months, started to develop a whole different mindset than before.

****

Tyrin couldn't believe what God had done for him on New Year's Day when he revived his daughter, Destin. He named her Destin because he knew that when death came, God had the final say-so. Her "destiny" was far greater than anyone had plans for. 'T was so over-protective of

his baby sister, and both him and Londyn were happy Journey had a playmate now. Tyrin was proud of his son making the decision to be a stand up young man in God. He admired him in a lot of ways and did not want to admit that The Lord was using his son to minister to him and call him out of darkness and into the path he set out just for him.

Bria remained in a coma through the month of January, but regained consciousness and finally her memory during the earlier parts of February. When she heard about Tyrin laying hands on their dead daughter, and the power of God raised her up, she became even more enamored with Tyrin and the hidden mysteries to this man.

While they both were relieved that their truth finally came to the surface and that they were the parents of a beautiful miracle baby, Bria's heart still ached for the heartbreak she caused her husband and boyfriend since they were seventeen years-old, Dearron Howard. He was indeed a good man. A godly man, and she only prayed that God would bless him tremendously for taking care of and being a support and her love for the years that he was. He helped groom her spiritually into the woman she was, and she wanted nothing but his approval over the years, however the approval was never supposed to be from 'D, but from Christ.

Anything you put before God becomes a curse to you and his Word was not mocked. In so many ways, Bria had lived for the Word of Dearron and his commands. What pleased him instead of what pleased God. She thanked God for getting this revelation of love right in front of her by way of Tyrin Williams. Going from being a Howard to stepping into the Williams namesake was a huge jump. Two totally different lanes and backgrounds, but with the help from The Lord this transition would be a smooth one.

****

There were no apologies greater than changed behavior, and in their case, he knew her behavior when it came to Tyrin was something more than she ever had the guts to admit to him. Dearron was so broken, he filed quickly, and divorced Bria quietly. Because she had enough respect for him and the son they created in love, they were able to work out a successful co-parenting plan. The only thing he had to make clear to Bria was to make sure that if she was to have Tyrin around 'Noah, that he never lay a hand on his son, and that the discipline only should come from him.

He announced to his congregation that he was going on a sixteen-month sabbatical to re-group spiritually as well as heal emotionally from the demise of the sixteen years that he was married to his ex-wife. His relationship with Christ was now his only priority, and he needed Him now more than ever if he even wanted to consider be a leader over God's people or over a family again in the future.

****

Kamal had only heard from his brother in Christ once—when he arrived safely at his destination in Phoenix, Arizona. His heart went out for him, but he had his own convictions and kinks to work out with his own relationship with Christ. While the Lord seemed to have healed his wife supernaturally, there were still some areas in which he knew he would have to be patient with her in. He worked hard every day to make sure she could feel secure with him and the life he was committed to giving her. He also knew he had to pray hard for the spirit of depression that forever tried to attach itself to her since the miscarriage. At one point she thought she might have had to take an anti-depressant but thank God she was able to fight a little harder to come out of the initial phase.

Since then, there was a period where they both wanted to try again, but when it came to them doing the do, he went limp and she became nervous. They knew that was God telling them, not time yet. Everything in his timing.

Pastor Samuels was so impressed and proud of the growth spiritually in Kamal and Ondrea's marriage, to the point he stepped aside and allow Kamal to take over as Pastor of Destiny to Faith Deliverance.

Ondrea had a smooth transition into the role of First Lady with the help of Bria. Although the saying went, "once a First Lady, always a First Lady." Bria laughed at that concept being that Tyrin was straight out the street and just trying to establish a credible name and legit business for himself. Ministry—church alone, was never a priority or focus for him in his life. There were the occasional women who gawked and stared her husband down whenever Kamal got up to preach on Sundays, however Ondrea knew how disciplined her husband was, and that he never missed a beat for five AM prayer after his workouts.

His new tattoo he had gotten across his chest, was praying hands with the scripture Luke 18:1- "Watch ye therefore and pray always, that you may be accounted worthy to escape all these things that shall come to pass, and to stand before the Son of man." Kamal knew the importance of prayer, and that even on a strong day, he had Ondrea on deck. As a man who dealt in extremes, he had to have her around him in case the Word he had hidden in his heart, ever was weak and might sin against it, she would be the visual to keep him on track.

Praying for women with those strong lust spirits was the main reason that he stayed prayerful the way he did. Because his personality dealt in extremes, Kamal knew that while he worked so hard to get from the worldly into the godly mindset he had now, he was not above falling from grace. Whenever it got too tough, Ondrea never knew it, but that's where he would call for her afterwards in his study and take her down right there. No woman he had been with prior ever felt like her. Their connection was definitely divine, and he would always be sure to protect it with his life and everything within his soul as he could.

He also stayed three steps ahead when it came to fight against the spirit of anger. Whenever he prayed for someone with this spirit, that's when he loved to watch comedies and play R&B and jazz songs all day to keep him in the headspace of love. For love is patient, kind and keeps no record of wrongdoings—especially when it came to his dealings with Tyrin. Kamal always had to fight the feeling of retribution for Chances murder—more importantly, he needed to finally forgive himself, and to leave that burden there, never to be picked up again. *But, what do you do when your past haunts you in your face forever?*

Chapter Seventeen

Sincere was on the road for the "Elite Eight" rounds in the NCAA Division I Men's Basketball Championship, and so far, their team was predicted to take the full tournament to become the national champions. Even though they just finished winning their first game of this round and in the middle of celebrating their victory, he wanted to check in with Tania and FaceTime after her surgery.

"Hey babe," he said as he perked up, cheesing hard after seeing her face on the camera.

"Hey," she said dryly.

"I can come back at another time," Sebastian whispered to Tania from her hospital doorway. She shook her head no and motioned for him to come and sit on the bed by her.

"What's the matter?" Sincere asked concerned. He knew the vibe was off between them but could not pick up why.

"I'm in a lot of pain, but again, I'm glad I went forward with the surgery."

"Aw, Sweet T, I wish I was there for you right now."

"No, you're good."

He didn't like the shortness in her conversation, "Is the background noise from my teammates bothering you or something? I can try and find someplace else to talk…"

"No, you're fine. Congrats on your win also, Sincere. I'm proud of you."

He needed to hear those words from her right about now. "Why thank you, baby. So, are you able to go home today or tomorrow?"

"Right now, the doctors are saying its looking like tomorrow because the goal is to get my pain under control."

"Okay, Tania...well, I want you to get some more rest and I'll be praying for that pain to get better for my baby."

"Sure thing...thanks, Sincere."

"I love you..."

"Love you too," she said with a hint of hurt in her voice.

"Bye."

Tania was highly upset that after her surgery, the only person who was there for her from start to finish was Sebastian. He even skipped school to be here. She loved Sincere, but she was hurt. Hurt that he didn't choose her at the time she needed him most.

"I wasn't trying to interrupt anything, Tania...just checking on you."

"No, I appreciate you thinking of me—especially when I haven't been exactly the most pleasant person to encounter since the accident."

Sebastian lowered his head in shame, "Trust me, you haven't offended me at all. I earned my punishment. I'm just glad it starting to end. The biggest slap in the face was seeing you in the hospital before, to the wheelchair, to crutches and now. I hate that I have been the catalyst for negative events in your life."

"It wasn't all bad, Sebastian," Tania returned with a smile.

"You mean that?"

"Yeah, outside of you trying to do me all the time, we had pretty good times," she replied while laughing.

He came closer to her, "that's because it was always so much chemistry there, on top of those kisses you gave," he said while staring at her full, pouty lips.

As Sebastian licked his lips seductively and moved even closer towards her face, Tania leaned forward, and then turned her head at the last minute when she realized what was about to happen.

"Listen Sebastian, we do have a chemistry because we were together just at the beginning of last year. You have to understand though that while I may be pissed at Sincere for my own reasons, I choose not to discuss with you, that doesn't mean I'm going to disrespect him in his absence. I have love for you, but not the kind enough to be a wife to you...only Sincere."

In that awkward space in time, one of the nurses came in to check on her, and next her mother and Kamal walked in to check on her.

"Hello Sebastian," they both said in unison.

"Hello Minister Kamal and Ms. 'Drea...I was just leaving."

"Thanks for checking up on her, and have a good day," Kamal added. He had begun to peep game the moment they came in the room, and knew what Sebastian was up to. Once he left out of the room, Kamal looked directly at Tania and told her to be careful.

Tania was so angry with Sincere she was not trying to hear or take heed to Kamal's warning.

****

"Good Morning, Saints of God! Happy Sunday...God is good!"

"Morning, Pastor," one member of the congregation called out.

"I recently encountered something very disturbing to me, and its how the enemy will try and come for us when our defenses are down.... defenses meaning focus, strength, the will to do God's Will and emotional health. I don't have a subject this morning, I just want to talk to you Saints on today."

"Talk to us, Sir!" Brother Bryan yelled out.

118

"Romans 12:2 states, '…And do not be conformed to this world: be ye transformed by the renewing of your mind, that ye may prove what is good, and acceptable, and perfect, will of God'…to conform means to be of similar form of type, or to comply with rules. Now we know God has established a set of rules for all of us to follow, from the pulpit to the doors out there," he said as he pointed towards the front doors of the church.

"In order to not be conformed to this world, the renewing of your mind starts when you do as in Philippians 3:13 & 14 verses…forgetting those former things you did while you were in the world in order to come into the new mind. You have to be so locked into the Lord that nothing and no one can penetrate your heart with some nonsense. Your heart is desperately wicked, how many by show of hands raised know this?"

He paused as only a handful of the congregation raised their hands.

"I see some of ya'll really need to go back to reading your Bibles…Jeremiah 17:9 clearly states: 'The heart is deceitful above all things, and desperately wicked; who can know it?' This is why its imperative to hear the Word and study the Word, so you'll know how to defeat the Word. When you go back up to Jeremiah 3:15, this is why he gives you pastors according to His heart—not according to what you think you need. Do you give your kids what they want all the time?"

A lot of people shook their heads no.

"Exactly…because you know what they need. Well, the Lord is just like that…its being brainwashed in a sense to His Will and His way. This is the beauty and mystery all at the same time of the God we serve. Always remember people of God, that He will lead and guide you like Bobby Brown, with 'every little step you take,' and that can start today if you ain't scared."

As soon as he looked back into the congregation upstairs in the overflow, he saw that Tyrin was visiting again this morning. He was still standing up from earlier with tears streaming down his face. "If you feel

119

the Lord tugging at your soul, harden not your heart and come to the altar of your heart to receive Jesus Christ as Your personal Lord and Savior...surrender that worldly heart for the new mind."

Without any reservations nor hesitation, Tyrin immediately made his way down the steps and towards the altar. He proceeded to kneel down, sobbing uncontrollably while repeating, "I'm sorry! I'm sorry!"

Kamal began to lay hands on Tyrin's forehead, and also kneeled to lay hands on his chest where his heart was. "Brother Tyrin, the Lord has heard you with your broken spirit and contrite heart long before you decided to make up in your mind to answer His call."

Kamal stood up to address the congregation as the Holy Spirit had its way in Tyrin as he began to speak in new tongues on the spot. "Ya'll see this? God has chosen this man from the beginning of the foundation of the world to serve Him and raise up a generation of strong soldiers in this Christian army...watch what I say and mark my words on this date."

Kamal had the men working the altar help Tyrin stand back up while he tried to speak to him again. "Brother, are you ready now? You can run, but you can't keep hiding. God allowed His resurrection power to flow through you to raise up your baby girl!" At the recollection of this miracle, Kamal couldn't help but begin to praise God and cut a shout himself. The church erupted into a Holy Ghost party, and Kamal went crazy with his praise. "The gates of Hell will not prevail! This man will shake up and help break the chains of bondage and Hell!"

Tyrin at that point began to run around the sanctuary and begin to shout. Something he had never done in his life. Kamal recognizing what was occurring in Tyrin's life before his own eyes smiled in awe of the transforming power of God. He knew that from this point in Tyrin's life, it would never be the same, and his elevation would be sudden, and that Tyrin would be able to move in the spirit supernaturally/. *He's called, Lord and I know now why You suffered for things to go down the way that You allowed. Only a God like that can maneuver the way You have. The*

Bad Boys of Gospel will be established, in Jesus' Name. You are worthy to be praised.

****

"What an awesome move of God this morning, Pastor," said Ondrea.

"To God be all the glory!" Kamal was still giving God the praise for all that he had done.

"Wait until 'Rin hears about what happened to his dad!" Tania exclaimed. It had been nine days since she had returned home, and she was already finding it a little easier to maneuver through the pain.

"Now, now baby girl, let Tyrin tell his son himself. That man is not the same from this day forward."

Ondrea turned on the news and saw Sincere on the television. "Hey guys, Sincere and his team are on the news! The Final Four games are this weekend coming up…look at our son-to-be," she beamed with pride.

Suddenly, Tania felt so much remorse for allowing Sebastian to get that close to her again. She was engaged. *I can't believe I was going to kiss him while Sincere is playing his heart out trying to secure us a future. Lord, forgive me.* She knew eventually she was going to have to confess her fault to him.

Chapter Eighteen

Sincere had flown her, and his family out to Caesar's Superdome in New Orleans for the final games, and Tania couldn't have been happier. Just to be able to not only use her cane, but also be able to be courtside to watch her man scratch, claw, scrape, and fight to dominate that basketball and execute three pointers with such precision up and down the basketball court doing what he loved, was worth it for her. Tania decided to support Sincere with whatever decision he made. He stayed prayed up as well, so she had to do like her stepfather advised them during the couple's class about trusting him to take the lead as he learns how to take lead from and follow Christ.

"And our NCAA Men's Basketball Division I Champions are the Temple University Owls!" the stadium erupted in cheers from thousands of people who came from far and wide to watch this heavily anticipated dance in collegiate sports events. As much as she wished she could run out onto the floor and jump up in his arms, she knew her limitations. Tania watched them cut the net down in victory, and for Sincere to hold up the trophy in all its glory.

While the reporters began their individual interviews, one from ESPN asked Sincere who he wanted to thank. "I have to thank my Lord and Savior, Jesus Christ, my parents, teammates, and this win is dedicated to the two most important women in my life...my late Grandmother Helen who passed this year, and my fiancée', Tania Williams. I love you, baby!"

Tania stood to her feet, feeling on like she was floating on Cloud Nine blowing him all kinds of kisses.

****

"Sincere, I owe you an apology…" Tania decided to admit her fault to him when he lay his head in her lap while they were chilling in the hotel room.

Sincere looked up at her from where he lay, "what's up?"

"I was so selfish and got mad at you when you couldn't be here for me after my surgery. I started letting Sebastian come and keep me company while I was in the hospital and he talked to me a couple times on the phone during that time…I'm so sorry, but I have everything cut off now, and I never did anything with him the entire time, I swear."

Sincere was quiet for a moment, and then sat up, taking her hands into his. "You didn't kiss him? Suck or 'F' him?"

Tania shook her head from left to right and replied, "No."

He then grabbed her face, "The we're all good, Sweet T. Again, I hate that I left you uncovered like that. Time that you may spend together with any dude don't mean anything to me if you know where you belong. I can't control you—not gonna try—how you move is how you move, but as long as you know me and you are 'home,' all these niggas can do is try." He then kissed her on the lips so passionately and aggressively, "they got nothing on it, trust me…this union is ordained by God."

"Make sure you keep that same energy if and when you enter the draft, Sir," Tania returned playfully.

"No need to worry your pretty little self, I got word the Detroit Pistons want me and they have the Number Two pick in the draft if I enter…that is if I have your blessing?"

"I guess I can apply to Oakland University in Auburn Hills…it's my cousin's alma mater," she said with a wink.

"Thank you, baby, I love you!" Sincere said returning his gratitude with another passionate kiss.

Epilogue

"Your moment is here brother...you ready?" Kamal asked as he prepared to walk in with Tyrin.

"Lord, be with me," he said nervously, as it was his first time stepping foot in the pulpit. Lord, *help me decrease so that You get all increase.*

"Oh, He kept me/ God kept me/ He kept me, so I wouldn't let go..." were the melodious words to Kurt Carr's song Sweet Wonder," sang by the choir that night. Ondrea sang right along with them remembering vaguely that this was the exact song being sung when she first laid eyes on her husband, now Pastor Kamal Davis. She looked down at her Apple watch to check the time. Service was to start soon. As soon as she looked back up, in walked Tyrin Sr. with Kamal, and with a Bible in his hand. She was pleased to recognize that same anointing that followed her husband was on Tyrin as well.

Bria couldn't help but smile at her husband and what God had done in not just his life, but for their family. She found that it was a little odd that he was walking out with a Bible—*maybe he's Kamal's new armor bearer* she thought to herself. Londyn, Jonoah and Destin were all smiles at Tyrin standing as a man of God. Bria looked over at 'T who sat in shock at just the sight of his father in a church, let alone carrying a Bible. *God, you really are amazing!*

After Kamal introduced Tyrin as Minister Tyrin Williams Sr. to the congregation and visitors, it became hard for Bria to keep her attention on the Word of God. She stared upfront in the direction of Ondrea, trying to catch her attention while she was sitting in the chair designated for the First Lady, but at that point in the service, Ondrea's attention was given to her husband while she watched him with a smile and adoration,

124

rubbing her seven-month pregnant and swollen belly, as he continued his remarks on Minister Williams.

Minister Williams then shook Kamal's hand and opened his Bible as he prepared to address the people.

"Please open up your Bibles, as well as your hearts to receive Habbakuk 2:2" he stated. "...and it reads 'And the Lord answered me and said, write the vision and make it plain upon tables that he may run that readeth it'...my thought on tonight is 'He Changed My Vision: This Clearly Wasn't That."

"Amen, to God be all the glory!" Kamal shouted in anticipation for what God was getting ready to set off when Tyrin delivered his message to drop a "Holy Ghost" bomb.

****

About the Author

Carrie B. Farley is a human services professional who received her master's degree in Human Services with a School Counseling specialization, and a bachelor's degree in Sociology with a Social Work Concentration. She loves reading, watching movies and playing The Sims. She resides in Ohio with her family.

Join Love Series Email List at Beautyfromashesllc44@gmail.com

Follow For Updates!!!!!

Website: beautyfromashes44.com

FB: @theloveseries44

IG: authorcarriefarley

Twitter: FarleyCarrie

Previous Books:

Love Chances

Love Changes: A Second Chance

Love Challenge

Beauty From Ashes: A Journey to Beauty